Beautiful Anna Raven

*

by

Matthew Kitsell

Story Consultant – Matthew J Gunn

My special thanks to

Kay, Peter, Carol, Mr G, and of course Mum, for all your kindness and support.

1

It was precisely six o'clock on the sixth day of October when Noonan passed the sign that stated, "Welcome to Denby". He had started his journey ten days ago with no real destination in mind and no plan beyond following his instincts and trusting his luck. Evening was starting to fall. He had been walking for nine hours, his stomach was beginning to ache with hunger, and he was grateful for the chance to rest up somewhere and eat something.

The road twisted upwards towards the crest of a hill. Noonan had no idea what sight would greet him when he reached the top, though he knew that he was close to the water. A fishing village? The gradient got steeper and the road seemed to narrow. He picked up his pace and made for the top of the hill. He would certainly find a Bed and Breakfast to settle down in overnight. Maybe he would stay a few days. He just did not know. As was always the case, he would move on when he knew it was time to do so.

Noonan belonged to no-one and no place. That was his way. And he kept moving. Everything that belonged to him was in his rucksack. There were few parts of the country that he had not been in and none that had been worth staying in. So, he had drifted towards the west country, the coast of North Devon. Beads of sweat started to form on his forehead and his thighs burned with the intensity of his brisk pace. And then finally he was at the top.

His eyes took in the view before him. It was like a painting. Bathed in the golden glow of the evening sun, Denby shimmered as if in a dream, smiling at him, inviting him in. The steeple of a church, stretching high above the buildings all around it, was caught in the sun. Beyond it, the wide stretch of the Bristol Channel, with the masts and dinghies of its boats gently bobbing in the evening breeze, sparkled with specks of gold. For a few moments, Noonan was back in the land of his childhood: golden evenings on the lawn outside the hotel; the thrill of the games that he played with the other children there... Quickly Noonan shook the memories out of his mind. Often people would get sentimental about the past, but Noonan saw no good in it. It only happened because the past was a place that could never be returned to. He had not given his childhood a moment's thought for many years. He was surprised and mildly ashamed of himself for having been weak enough to allow it back in now. Nonetheless, something about that first impression of Denby had cut right through to him. He walked down the hill quickly.

He passed the first set of buildings and reached a crossroads. An elderly couple with a dog nodded a curt greeting and passed on quickly. He was used to the suspicious glares he occasionally received from locals. He understood how he must have appeared to them. He did not care. And he did not blame them. Days of being on the road had left him with an unkempt, slightly wild appearance. Well, a bath and a shave would soon take care of that. Feeling his thighs burning and his stomach aching with hunger, Noonan marched towards the open door of the local public house. Already Noonan was imagining the warm, soothing taste of real ale as it washed down his throat and into his stomach. The building was coated in black paint and must have been at least two centuries old. A sign above the

7

window told him that he was entering "The Chequered Flag".   He walked in.

The interior of the pub was dimly lit, and Noonan had the impression of shuffling and coughing as he entered.   His eyes adjusted to the darkened interior.   He was suddenly aware of a small dog sniffing his feet.   He looked down to see a small poodle and then up into the weathered face of the owner.   He did not care for dogs.   He took in the straggly grey hair and deep brown eyes of the old man.   The old man chuckled and muttered something that Noonan was not able to understand. Noonan moved away from him and walked up to the bar.

The woman behind the bar was clearly edging past fifty.   Her clear, aquamarine eyes and thick auburn hair tied up in a bun immediately gave the appearance of an attractive woman that time was now playing its dirty tricks on. Flecks of grey hair stubbornly showed behind her ears and the skin around her eyes were developing that oddly pasty look common in women her age who perhaps did not look after themselves as well as they might.   The woman in turn took in the unkempt stranger standing before her. When he had entered a moment ago, she had instantly sized him up as one of the drunks from one of the neighbouring towns down the road. She did not recognise him, but he seemed to fit the profile. Occasionally they would stagger in, make a nuisance of themselves, then mercifully spill out into the street, hopefully never to return. Yet there was something elegant and authoritative in the stranger's purposeful walk that did not fit that image. He seemed to own the space around him as he moved. There was a calm confidence in his walk, a dangerous lethargy. Was he going to be a different kind of troublesome customer? But then when he lifted his head and looked her directly in the face, she was surprised yet again. The bright, clear grey eyes held hers with a warmth and curiosity that she had not expected. They seemed to be smiling at her. His long, thick, chestnut brown hair hung loosely, messily over his ears. His clothes were the sort bought at an army surplus store: a green camouflage jacket and a cheap pair of faded jeans. He would have seemed entirely unremarkable, but the woman could see nothing now except the man's eyes, which continued to take her in.

"What'll you have, love?"

Noonan looked along the row of taps. He smiled back at the woman.

"Pint of ale, please."

His voice was unexpectedly quiet, thoughtful, like a college lecturer or a surgeon. Noonan reached into his pocket and took out a thick brown wallet. He pulled out a crisp, new pound note and held it out to the woman. She noticed then that his hands were like an animal's paws with a lot of scars and scabs. If he had been living rough, that might explain those. She picked up a glass and filled it with the thick, amber liquid. The froth rose quickly to the top of the glass and spilled over. Noonan licked his lips in relish. The woman came back and put the heavy glass down, taking the still-offered pound note.

"Seventy, love."

She went to the cash register and came back a moment later with his change. She dropped the coins into his hand.

"Thank you." The woman turned to go. "Do you have any rooms?" Noonan asked.

"Three," nodded the woman. "All available. You're lucky it's off-season. You wouldn't have stood a chance in the summer."

"How much?"

"Seven pounds fifty." She looked at him doubtfully, as though this might be enough to change his mind. Instead, Noonan merely shrugged.

"Fine." Noonan lifted the glass to his lips and took a long pull at it. He closed his eyes, luxuriating in the soft, bitter taste. The liquid instantly warmed his stomach and gave him a feeling of strength, as it always did. "Is there a barber's? Or a second-hand clothes shop?"

"High street's down the end of the road, turn left. You should find everything you need there."

Noonan smiled and nodded. "Thank you. I'll have a look around once I've finished my drink. And then perhaps I could see the room?"

"Of course – take all the time you need."

The woman smiled at him again. This time however Noonan could see that the smile was a genuine one. This would be a good place for him. The woman turned and walked off down the bar. Noonan pulled up a stool and sat on it. For the next few minutes, he allowed the ale to work its magic. He glanced around the room at the other customers. He concluded that if you walked into any public house at this time of day anywhere in the country you would find the equivalent of this exact crowd sitting there: an older, grey haired fellow with an enormous grey, shaggy beard and a thick sweater, sitting hunched over his evening newspaper at his own table in the corner; two ravaged-faced locals, scruffy in ripped jeans with two days' worth of stubble, smoking roll-up cigarettes; two more respectable looking women in their fifties, smartly dressed with white wines, one leaning forward and speaking intently while the other listened and occasionally nodded her head; a young female assistant, aged about nineteen, flitting back and forth with trays of food; a bored looking man of about thirty, scowling over the rim of his beer glass; and the man with the dog. In this company Noonan figured he would not appear out of place at all.

It took roughly twenty minutes for Noonan to thoroughly drain his glass. He abhorred waste of any kind. He nodded to the woman behind the bar and stood up.

Noonan walked to the door and out onto the narrow street. The chill of the evening breeze coming off the water gently stroked his forehead. He strolled down to the waterfront.   A promenade stretched out before him.   A row of small dinghies and rowing boats bobbed up and down gently in the water. Noonan walked to the edge of the promenade, where a low wall separated the pavement from a much deeper drop into the water.   Noonan stepped up onto the wall and looked out across one of the most magnificent seascapes he had ever seen. The evening sun sat on the horizon like a bright, orange beach ball, cutting a long shimmering path of light along the surface of the water. Two boats drifted idly miles out on the horizon. Noonan momentarily lost himself in the peace and majesty of the scene before him.   His thoughts started drifting back to his childhood again and he instantly turned them off.   Forcing himself to focus, he made a bet with himself that the sun would disappear completely in twenty minutes and suddenly jumped back off the wall and walked along the promenade.

Noonan was eight minutes out – it took only twelve minutes for the sun to drop behind the edge of the world.   There was a smattering of evening strollers, visitors and dog walkers also out enjoying the evening.   Suddenly wanting to be away from everyone, Noonan turned down a footpath heading back inland. After passing the back gardens of various cottages, the path took a half-turn to the right and he was suddenly climbing again, passing banks of freshly cut grass on both sides. At the top of the hill was the church he had seen earlier with the steeple proudly towering over everything around it. The gradient was steep, and Noonan found himself jogging up it to make the going easier. A few seconds later, he was walking towards a gate that led into the church yard. He pushed it away from him and saw that he was in a small graveyard. Noonan always liked to visit the churches of any town or village that he was passing through. Churches were private, peaceful sanctuaries from which the chaos and craziness of the world outside could be kept at bay. Therefore, it always annoyed him intensely whenever he found that church doors had been locked – it seemed so antithetical to the whole purpose of churches.

He stepped up to the church door and was happy to find that it opened for him. The church was from the Norman period and had a musty smell of incense and old stone. The nave stretched to five pews leading to the altar.   So far, so normal.   What did not strike Noonan as normal however was the scene playing out in front of the altar.   Three other people were facing each other and seemingly engaged in a fierce argument.   On the right were two men: one overweight, about forty years of age, a brute, with puffy cheeks and greasy hair, wearing a soiled leather jacket; the other, a craggy reptile of a man with clumpy, stringy hair and an awkward, loping gait.   The brute was hissing angrily through his teeth to the third member of the party standing apart from them on the left, a wholesome, attractive young woman, wearing a smart pair of jeans and an elegant grey sweater. She looked pale and frightened. The brute was obviously furious about something but was nonetheless trying to keep his voice down as if in respect to his surroundings. The reptile said nothing, just stared at the young woman, a horrible leer on his face. The young woman was shaking her head desperately at the brute.   From where he was, Noonan could make out no words.   It quickly became apparent that his entrance into the church had gone unnoticed by all three of them.   Noonan had no interest in the petty quarrels of strangers and on any other occasion would have discreetly let himself out of the church and let them get on with it. But then something happened that made that an impossible course of action for him. The girl suddenly summoned the courage to shout back at the brute, "You tell him I'm finished with him! With all of them! And then you can both crawl into your little holes and bury yourselves in them!" The girl had barely managed to get the last word out before the brute lifted his right hand and slapped her hard across the face. Shocked, the girl took a couple of steps back and brought her hand up to her face. The reptile just watched the display in quiet amusement. The brute moved in to strike at her again, but the girl scrambled out of the way. It was then that she turned and saw Noonan standing in the doorway. She gave a gasp. Following her gaze, the brute and the reptile also turned to Noonan and froze. The brute dropped his fist and stood limply, as if a guilty secret of his had just been let out. Noonan, his face revealing nothing, just stood there and took him in. The girl, her face flushed with relief, took the opportunity to move quickly to Noonan's side. Raising himself back to his full height, the brute started to walk slowly, menacingly towards Noonan. The reptile continued to leer, but a look of curiosity had now crept into his face.

"You're in the wrong place, mate. I suggest you piss off out of here. Now."

The reptile briefly laughed chokingly.

Noonan nodded. His answer was slow, measured. "Wrong place – right time. From the look of things."

"You hear what I said?" The brute's voice hardened, finding its confidence again.

"I'll go only if the young lady wants me to. You don't count."

The brute's face suddenly darkened to an ugly shade of crimson. Noonan turned to the young woman and gave her a look of assurance. Her eyes sent him a message, which he understood. The brute raised a finger at Noonan, pointing it directly at his forehead.

"You've just got yourself in a lot of trouble, pal," he hissed at him menacingly. "I'm giving you a chance to get out of here now. But if I ever see you again, you're going to be spending a long time in hospital. You understand, you stupid vagrant bastard?"

"Mind your language," Noonan rebuked him. "Remember where you are."

The brute's eyes flashed furiously.

Noonan continued, "If we're lucky, neither of us will have to see *you* again."

At this, the brute suddenly took a step back and threw his fist forward towards Noonan's face. It was a clumsy, poorly co-ordinated punch and Noonan had expected it. He stepped to one side, moving the girl out of the way. Then Noonan elegantly moved in and his fist shot forward like a piston, right into the brute's nose. The look of fury was instantly replaced by a look of bewilderment and shock. Blood shot out of his nose. His heavy body tumbled backwards several feet, crashing into the neatly ordered rows of wooden seats. He collapsed to the ground, pulling several of the chairs down with him. The sounds of the chairs falling echoed around the old building. Noonan looked up at the reptile, who now looked bewildered and mortified. Nonetheless he plucked up his courage and rushed towards him. Noonan side-stepped him and planted a firm punch on the side of his face, which sent him flying into the wall. His body sunk to the ground.

Noonan lowered his arm and turned back to the girl. "Come on, let's get you home," he said quietly. They turned and walked quickly out of the church.

"That should keep them occupied for a while," Noonan assured her.

It was only once they had cleared the little gate that led into the graveyard that the girl finally spoke. In a throaty whisper, she said, "Thank you," and after that it was not until they had got to the bottom of the hill that she spoke again.

"My name's Anna. What's yours?"

<u>2</u>

"Dennis. Dennis Cavell." He had got used to introducing himself as such and no longer needed to remind himself to do so. To an extent, even he was beginning to believe he was Dennis Cavell. Certainly, it was an ordinary name, and the girl would not give it a second thought. Noonan walked briskly. He did not want to make any more conversation with this girl than he had to. If she was in any kind of trouble, that was her business. People in bad situations came to them through decisions they had made about their own lives, or people they had chosen to associate with. Noonan was only concerned with his own situation in life. He had got this girl, Anna, out of a nasty situation, and was glad to have done so. But he would get her safely away and then she would be on her own.

"Are they following?" The girl looked to him for reassurance. Noonan turned his head.   They were back by the water now.   No-one was behind them.

"No, there's no-one."

They walked to the low wall. Darkness was fast approaching now but there was still a golden glow on the horizon.

"Are you a visitor here, Anna?   Or do you live here?" Noonan asked.

Anna shrugged.   "I've been here for nine months now."   She looked out for a moment across the water then suddenly turned back to him.   "Look, thank you for what you did back there.   If you hadn't come when you did...."

"Do they know where you live?"

"No.   I mean, I don't think so."

"Do you live near here?"

She nodded.   "I'm renting one of the little cottages down by the harbour.   Why?"

"Well, this is a tiny village.   How long do you think it's going to take them to find you again?   If you know anyone well here, I'd stay with them for the next few days.   And if they do find you again you may have to speak to the police."

They walked on in silence for a while and it was starting to make Noonan feel uncomfortable.   To get around this, he suddenly found himself offering, "I'll see you to the front door, if you like."

She looked at him, surprised. There was a moment's hesitation before she answered, "Thank you. I'd appreciate that."

A chill was blowing in from the water now and there were fewer people about. A young, dishevelled couple with a lumbering Labrador tripped past them. Noonan could hear their giggles drifting away into the evening wind. Noonan glanced at Anna and took her in properly for the first time. Pink still showed in her left cheek from where the brute had struck her, but that aside she was unmarked. She was a beautiful girl, willowy and with an aristocratic hauteur that came over strongly in her confident walk. Her hair was the colour of flames, with streaks of blond in the upper layers, which was swept back on her head to the nape. It danced lazily in the evening wind. She was around five foot eight, with large, inquisitive, keenly observant green eyes and prominent cheek bones. She reminded Noonan of a lioness. Everything about her walk, her height and her features exuded worldliness and confidence. She looked like the PA to the

CEO of a global enterprise. She would own a luxury flat in one of the more desirable districts of London and possibly share it with a similarly successful partner. So, what was she doing in a small fishing village like this? And what kind of trouble had she gotten herself into? Noonan was not particularly curious to find out but would be happy to see her safely home. Then he would get back to the inn and settle down for a long, restful evening. Already he was looking forward to a long, hot bath with soapy water lapping around his aching muscles. Yes, it was going to feel good! He would sort this girl out and head back without further ado.

The buildings receded and an avenue of trees stretched out ahead of them. The lush smell of the evening hung pleasantly in the air. Noonan's thighs were aching, and he was feeling the twenty miles he had already walked that day. He hoped that they did not have much further to go. A tranquil lane veered off to the half-left and Noonan had a strong hunch that they had arrived. Anna quietly said, "I live just down here. I should be OK now."

"Are you sure?"

"Yes. Thank you so much once again."

"Goodbye, then."

"Bye..."

Noonan smiled, turned, and walked away. Just then the girl called out behind him.

"Sorry..."

Noonan turned.

"Erm..." She waved a hand. "Do you live around here?"

"Just arrived today."

"Holiday?"

Noonan shrugged, "Just passing through."

"Staying long?"

"A couple of nights, maybe three."

"Are you staying in the town?"

"I'll be at the inn."

"Well... Maybe I'll see you again?"

Noonan smiled. "Maybe." Anna turned and walked down the lane. For a moment Noonan watched the poised, confident back of the girl as she walked purposefully down the lane. Her posture and demeanour had changed since their first meeting, when she had almost shrunk back into the shadows of the church. Noonan watched her pass the first two cottages. Then she turned a corner and was suddenly gone. Noonan turned then and began the journey back.   Dusk was creeping out of the landscape now and the shadows were reaching out to him.   He thought of his bath again, then wondered why he had waited a few moments to watch the girl, Anna, walk away.   Had he been – despite all his supposed feelings to the contrary – genuinely concerned for the girl's safety? Certainly, he could sense that she was in serious trouble.   Had he been interested to know exactly which cottage was hers? Should he have taken her to the front door, just to be certain?   Had she in fact even made it to the front door?   Noonan forcefully told himself that he was being silly.   This was not his business.   And it was vital – always vital for his own sake – never to get mixed up in anyone else's business.   He picked up his pace, suddenly keen to get back to the warm inn and away from the creeping shadows...

The warmth and murmuring of voices seemed to embrace Noonan as he walked into the inn.   The fire in the corner sparked and crackled.   The old beardy fellow sitting on his own from earlier had acquired a similar, old beardy companion, and they were sitting at a table right in front of it with semi-bored expressions on their faces. The pub was fuller now and Noonan cast a quick glance round at all the faces. They all fit. All except two. And these were two faces he had hoped he would never have to see again.

Noonan and the brute's eyes caught each other at the same time. The brute's rapidly moving mouth suddenly froze. The reptile turned and followed his companion's gaze. They both fixed Noonan with mean, challenging stares. Dried blood hung from the left nostril of the brute. Noonan quickly turned away and waited at the bar for service. The landlady was now hard at work. Her head was fussily bobbing up and down as she poured pints and grabbed at packets of peanuts. Noonan could feel the eyes of the brute and the reptile boring through the back of his head. He was annoyed to find them there. On the other hand, it was a likely place for them to be, after all, in this tiny village. They might even have a room booked upstairs. Eventually – after what seemed an uncomfortable amount of time – the landlady turned to him.

"Ready to see your room now, love?"

"Yes, please."

"No problem, I'll get your key."

Six keys hung on hooks. She grabbed at the one on the end.

"I'll put you in number three, love. End of the corridor, on the left."

"That's great, thank you."

She smiled in response and quickly turned away. Noonan walked through a wooden door and up a dangerously steep flight of stairs. He turned left at the top and found his room at the end. Noonan was tall, six foot two, and the height of the hall was all of that. Noonan unlocked the door and went inside. The musty smell of home hit him immediately. The room was immaculate and cosy, with a kettle by the bed. It was perfect.

Noonan looked inside the bathroom, which contained just a shower unit. He disliked shower units because they always seemed to be more complicated than they needed to be. Mercifully, he had no trouble with this one and the water came out to his satisfaction straight away. Noonan quickly undressed and got under the warm, soothing jets of water. Steam quickly started to drift towards the ceiling. Noonan's body was wiry and lean like an animal. A glaring, gaping red wound just above his heart showed against his skin like an angry

27

beacon.   He immediately thrust his torso out so that the wound would be hit by the water straight away.   As always, the sting shot through him like a blade.   He hissed in pain.   Then, after only a few seconds, it subsided, and he felt fine.   He went through this every time he bathed or showered – always better to get that part out of the way first.

Fifteen minutes later, after a deliciously luxurious shower, Noonan was back in the room with a towel wrapped around him.   It took him only a few moments to dry himself thoroughly.   Then he turned the light out.   He walked to the window and closed the curtains.   He froze for a second.   Immediately beneath him, out in the street, looking up at him through the window, were the brute and the reptile. They just stared up at him.   A slow, ugly smile spread across the brute's face. Noonan closed the curtains, shook his head, and went back to the door.   He locked it.   Then he sunk gratefully into bed, pulled the sheets over him and closed his eyes.   The waves of sleep soon washed over him, and he was gone.

3

The demons came to visit Noonan during the night, as they often did. It was always the same scene every time. Wherever his unshackled mind wandered in his sleep, it always ended up back on the windy, black beach.

The beach. The blackness. The full moon cutting a long silvery path along the surface of the water. The harsh, black grit of the sand. The man – what remained of the man – crawling inch by bloody inch down towards the distant lap of the water. Dried, black blood caked across his back. The broken stubs of the fingers. The eyes – black, unseeing holes in the skull – staring desperately out towards the soothing lap of the water, the water that never seemed to get any closer. And then the cruel, unceasing laughter of the four men. The incessant, rhythmic lashing of the sticks in their hands. The man could feel every strike of the sticks even before they came down. There was no end to it. In the end, the man could crawl no further.

He simply rolled over onto his back and waited for the end.   His swollen eyes opened a fraction.   All he could see were the hooded heads of his tormentors, and the whites of their eyes gleaming devilishly at him.   The world suddenly became a blur.   It was always at this very point that the dream ended.

Noonan opened his eyes.   He was glad to be away from them and back in his hotel room.   Noonan had a body clock which had the uncanny knack of waking him up at 6.30 every morning.   When he was travelling, he would snap his body to attention and prepare himself for the journey that lay ahead that day.   Today he had no travelling to do, but laziness was something that Noonan could abide in no man, least of all himself.   Purpose and movement defined his whole character. Therefore, he was immediately out of bed and pulling his clothes on.   As he checked the meagre contents of his rucksack – a waterproof, an extra pair of trousers, extra T-shirt, his wallet which contained no cards but £50.00 in notes and a toothbrush - he started to form a plan.   He would start the day by finding a Barber's and he would smarten himself up.   Perhaps buy a fresh set of clothes, try to look less like a vagrant. His eventual purpose was to find a place to settle down, live quietly, anonymously. A place where he would be left alone. Noonan caught himself smiling in the mirror. That happy thought had made him think of good, strong coffee.

He arrived in the dining room to find it empty, which pleased him. Noonan liked to eat alone and savour his meals. For him, meals were one of the most precious luxuries of life. The idea of having to make forced conversation with other guests appalled him, so he was glad to find that he would be eating alone. Cereals, bread, milk and steaming pots of tea and coffee had already been laid out. Noonan walked over to the table and helped himself to black coffee. He found the table furthest away from the dining room door and sat down. He put the cup to his lips. The door to the dining room suddenly opened and the landlady strode boldly into the room. From her bright demeanour and energy, Noonan guessed that she had been up for at least two hours. She was wearing a white chef's top and a good-morning smile.

"You're early," she beamed at him. Noonan lowered his cup back onto its saucer, smiled and nodded. "Full English?"

"Thank you. And would you have some fruit as well?"

"Of course," she continued to beam while making a mental note. There was something almost insincere to Noonan about the enthusiasm of her hospitality, but he was fine with it. She turned to go.

"Is there anywhere I can go for a haircut?" Noonan asked this before she disappeared through the door. She turned.

"Well, there's Rene's at the end of the high street."

"Rene's..." Noonan committed the name to memory.

"That's it." The smile again. "Just give me a shout if there's anything you need."

Noonan nodded his thanks and the landlady left him to enjoy his breakfast. When the vegetarian breakfast came it was particularly good – the mushrooms were crisp but not burned and the sausages were cooked exactly right. He finished his breakfast just as a young couple entered the dining room, the first of the other guests to arrive for breakfast. It was half past seven. The young man had the lean look of a cycling enthusiast, with cropped hair and a wiry frame. His partner was young, blond, equally lean, but instantly forgettable. Noonan imagined that there was more fat to be found on their bicycles. He nodded at them and they smiled back. It was time to get moving. Noonan put his plate to one side and left the room.

A few minutes later Noonan was brushing through the door of the inn and stepping out onto the high street. The blessed warmth of the morning sun hit him like smile. It was a heavenly autumn day with a sky of the deepest blue. The lift that Noonan felt in his spirit was immediately dampened by the sight of the brute and the reptile huddled in a shop doorway on the other side of the street. As soon as they saw Noonan, they straightened up and tossed their cigarettes away. They were like two ugly warts on the face of a civilised community. Noonan's mind kicked in and started working. He was obviously of some importance to these two thugs, enough for them to hang around all night and wait for him. But why? He had stopped the brute from hurting Anna, but that was all he had done. In every other way, he was entirely unconnected to them. And what was their plan? It was clear that they were still looking for Anna and for some reason they saw him as an obstacle. Either that or they just had a score to settle. They were clearly waiting for an opportunity to get him alone. The brute had a carrier bag in his hand, possibly from a supermarket. It looked as though it contained a heavy item, possibly more than one. This presumably was a personal indulgence before the more serious business of looking for Anna continued. So, these two were amateurs – no serious professional would allow something as trivial as what took place the previous evening to get in the way of business. Whatever that business happened to be.

Noonan walked as though he had not noticed his pursuers, but he marked their positions in his mind, behind him and to the left. Rene's was exactly where the landlady had told him it would be. It was now eight o' clock. Noonan walked quickly inside, noticing the sharp 'ting' of the bell as he opened the door. Two young men in their early twenties, both with heavy stubble, looked up from their seats. They both had bored expressions on their faces and were in no hurry. One of them casually shuffled off his chair and looked up at Noonan with indifference. He waved Noonan to one of the chairs facing a mirror.

"Over here, please, boss," he murmured. Noonan sat himself down and looked at the unkempt face staring back at him. "And what are we doing for you today?"

"Shave and a tidy up, please."

"No problem." The barber, who did not look like a Rene, started to run his fingers through Noonan's hair. He leaned over and picked up a water sprayer. Noonan could feel the mist of water landing on his face, cooling it for a second. Then, having dampened his hair, the barber started to snip expertly at it. Chunks started to drop to the floor and Noonan immediately started to feel unburdened. The faces of the brute and the reptile briefly appeared in the mirror. They were watching him through the window. The barber made no attempt at conversation.

"Are they local?" Noonan asked.

"What?"

"Those two outside?"

The barber casually looked around, taking them in. "Never seen them before. Why?"

"How long have you been living here?"

"Grew up here.   You here on holiday?"

"Just passing through."

"Where are you heading?"

"Exeter."

There was no truth in this, but the answer achieved what Noonan wanted it to, which was to finish that part of the conversation.   Exeter would have been of no interest to the young barber.   Noonan gazed back in the mirror at the two outside.   Eventually they casually sauntered across the street.   The two of them lapsed back into silence.   It took twenty-five minutes to transform Noonan with a haircut and a shave.   He admired himself in the mirror.   He already looked ten years younger.   His grey eyes glittered fiercely back at him and his dark blond hair had been arranged tidily.   He was pleased.

"That'll be two pounds, please." Noonan reached into his wallet and took out two notes, handing them to the barber.

"Thank you."

Noonan looked across the street. The brute and the reptile.   It was time to deal with them now.   As he had been watching the clumps of hair falling away from his head, he had been working out his plan, which was perfectly straightforward. He picked up his rucksack, walked to the door and opened it. He ignored the two across the street and walked hurriedly away, going through in his mind what he was going to do.

4

Noonan was looking for open country. Somewhere as deserted as possible, away from hikers and dog walkers. He had turned inland. He had remembered footpaths going off from the main road on the way into the village. He had seen forestry rising from the valley on the other side of the hill. That was what he needed. Noonan kept up a brisk pace. He dared not risk a glance back at the brute and the reptile. He did not want to let them know that he was on to them. That would affect their behaviour and he wanted them feeling relaxed and confident. Noonan had a sixth sense for knowing when he was being followed. He did not need to look behind to know that the men were there. He could feel them there. They would be taking their time, relaxing.

The local dog walkers were already out. Noonan exchanged smiles with some of them. The sun was rising quickly in the sky and already Noonan started to feel sweat building on his forehead. It was a tough hill and the two behind him would take it slowly, dropping a few feet behind him. Noonan reached the crest of the hill and took the slope at a gentle pace. He took a corner and found what he was looking for. He had marked it in his head when he had arrived the previous evening – a footpath leading up into the hills. At the top of the hills were woods. Noonan took the path and knew that it would be impossible for his two pursuers to miss him taking it.

Nobody else was on the path. Wooden fences stretched away on both sides. Noonan stopped and leaned on the right-hand fence, staring down into the valley. To anyone watching, he was a walk leader from a local ramblers' society, perhaps practicing a route for a weekend meet. He inclined his head slightly to the right. Out of the corner of his eye, he could see the two figures starting up the path after him. Noonan resumed his climb. He needed to get to the woods quickly. When he reached the top of the hill, the footpath forked. Straight ahead of him was a stile leading into some woods. He vaulted over this and quickly disappeared into the trees.

The brute and the reptile arrived at the top of the hill about five minutes later. They had broken into a run as soon as Noonan's figure had disappeared into the woods. Noonan watched from behind a tree. The brute and the reptile were looking into the woods and speaking in low voices. The brute reached into his plastic bag and took out two thick iron bars, handing one to the reptile. The brute took a step back and swung his bar through the air. He nodded and smirked at the reptile. The brute pointed into the woods, the reptile nodded, and they climbed the stile. Noonan gently lowered himself to the ground, watching. The brute and the reptile were moving forward carefully. The brute walked in front, the reptile following thirty feet behind, both with their iron bars swinging from the hands. A skinny footpath snaked its way through the trees and the two of them stuck to it. Low branches and brambles scratched at their faces. The path had become overgrown and had evidently fallen out of favour with local walkers.

When the explosion of movement came it was over in an instant. Then the world was suddenly calm again, with just the sound of the wind gently swaying the branches of the trees. In that instant, a dark shadow had sprung out of the foliage, grabbed the reptile, and pulled him back into the foliage. The reptile did not even have time to call out. A firm hand clamped itself over his mouth and the reptile felt himself being dragged through the earth. Then suddenly the sky fell in on him and he was swimming in blackness.

The brute suddenly spun around, alerted by a noise that he had not been able to interpret. His companion was no longer behind him.

"Eddie?" he called out hoarsely.

No answer. The trees and the foliage stared back at him indifferently. A dog barked somewhere off to the left. The wind sounded in the trees.

"Eddie? What's up with you?" His hoarse, ugly voice cut through the woods. Still there was no reply from Eddie.

The brute jogged back along the path, looking from left to right, but there was no sign of his companion or the stranger. He was almost back at the stile, so he turned and started jogging back, panic rising in his stomach. Still there was no sign. He jogged all the way down the path, hoping to catch a glimpse of either Eddie or the other man. The path became thornier and more overgrown. Branches smacked him in the face.

"Eddie!"

Then suddenly he was at the end of the woods and a stile led away across a wide, empty valley. The brute looked out across the valley, confused and increasingly anxious. The iron bar was starting to weigh heavily in his hand.

He spent the next half hour going back and forth along the footpath, convincing himself that Eddie was going to appear before him, smirking something along the lines of "Sorry about that, mate, call of nature". But he knew deep down that he was never going to. What had really been bothering him was that the stranger had disappeared along with him. That was bad news. He was struggling to understand the sudden fear that he was feeling in his gut. For all his years of knocking around in dingily lit pubs, alleyways, pushing people around for information, he had never quite understood the fear of being alone in the woods. Finally, his patience snapped. He would go back to the village and concentrate on finding the girl. When

Eddie finally showed up, he would tell him exactly what he thought of him.   So, he walked back to the entrance of the wood and climbed the stile.

And then he froze.

A bloody bundle was blocking his way.

Eddie.

He would never have realised it, but his hand instantly went up to his throat in shock.   Someone – the stranger - had carefully propped Eddie's bloody and beaten body up against the fence.   Dried blood hung messily from the nostrils and the stomach rose and fell under laboured breathing.   Eddie was conscious but clearly dizzy.   Without quite realising it, the brute let the iron bar clatter to the ground.

"Eddie?"

The name came out softly, almost tenderly.   He felt shocked and ashamed. He had not intended for this to happen. This one was down to him.

A voice answered.   But it was not Eddie.   It sounded from behind him; it was a casual, friendly voice that carried a quiet authority.

"I could do the same thing to you very easily. But I don't think that's going to be necessary. Do you?"

The brute turned, his hand going for the switchblade in his pocket. He saw the stranger standing three feet behind him. The stranger's arm came up, grabbed the brute's wrist, and twisted it, snapping it as though it were a dried twig. The brute yelled out and dropped the switchblade, which landed in the grass with a thump.

"You broke my wrist! You bastard!"

"You followed me up here to do much the same to me. You'll be alright. Though I would avoid getting into any fights for a while."

The brute looked at him, his expression a mixture of helplessness and hatred. He searched for the right, venomous words to say. But no words ever came. The stranger just looked calmly at him, smiling almost angelically.

"Now start walking, all the way back to the village. And when you get there, get your things together and go. Because when I get back there, I don't expect to see you." He paused. "You understand, don't you?"

The brute rubbed his hand.

"If I ever see you again, you're dead. You get me?" he whimpered.

The words were there, but nothing in the voice could back them up. The smile on the stranger's face did not change. Miserably, the brute turned and started walking back down the hill, whining in pain as he went. Noonan stood and watched. The brute managed one final, filthy look behind him. Soon he was at the bottom of the hill and his figure disappeared. Noonan was alone with the unlucky Eddie. He quickly glanced down at him.

"Never mind, mate. You're better off out of it anyway – whatever it is."

Eddie groaned and moved his head. He appeared to be nodding. Noonan stepped away and was suddenly gone. Eddie looked around as far as his wounds would allow, but he could no longer see or hear him. There was just the wind in the trees and the distant sound of cars heading into the village.

5

The car park was a depressing place. In fact, describing it as a car park afforded the place a grandeur that it did not deserve. It was really a mud patch surrounded by a scrappy wire and wood fence. An old shed used to store tools stood at the entrance, its windows caked in dust and grime. Hardly anyone parked here. The land was dying a slow and grisly death. But Lee Mitchell knew that there was hope in this place. Within two years a brand new, state-of-the-art sports centre would cover the ground that stretched away all around him. On the site where his Mercedes was parked would be an altogether different kind of car park: tarmacked, properly maintained, modern. The glum, grisly spectacle of urban decline and decay was about to get a face-lift. And Lee Mitchell, Director of one of the largest and most profitable building conglomerates in the UK, Bamford Bowers, was the man who had been handed the contract to oversee the project. Mitchell sat in the back of his Mercedes and waited for the arrival of his business associate, Jimmy Jarrett, or, as he was often referred to in certain circles, Jimmy the Hit Man. Many associates he met in the boardroom or out on site. Jimmy, he only ever met in this place, an arrangement that both men adhered to strictly. Nobody except the two of them knew of their meetings. And no-one ever saw them, which was the reason that Mitchell had selected the car park. It was always deserted.

Mitchell looked away into the distance at the rising towers of Brentford, stretching up into the sky, desperately courting swanky modernity and failing ignominiously. Mitchell was confident that a similar fate would never befall his sports centre. None of Mitchell's buildings ever fell short of the mark. That was how he had earned and kept his reputation, a builder who could take the grubbiness of the present and transform it into the sparkle of the future. He had done it every time up to now and he would do it again. What was the expression he had heard recently that summed up everything he believed? "There's nothing more dated than yesterday's future". Yes, that was the secret – never to follow trends. Trends go out of fashion very quickly and are then sneered at. The secret to the buildings that grow in respectability is that they follow classical, simple styles. Unlike the ugly chimneys that stretched away into the horizon on his left.

Mitchell lifted the cigarette to his mouth and took a log pull. He let the smoke lazily drift through his teeth and out of the open car window. Then, the cigarette nearly down to the butt, he casually flicked it out of the window. He picked up a small transistor radio that was by his side and twisted the switch. With a burst of crackle, the sounds of "'60s Merseybeat" filled the car. Mitchell had the radio tuned to Radio 2 and it would stay tuned to Radio 2. He was only interested in the good stuff. And the good stuff had happened ten, fifteen years ago. Unlike buildings, it seemed, popular music had died somewhere along the way and there was no hope for it. But there would always be the classics, so it mattered little. He would never have realised it, but his fingers were drumming along to the cheery sounds of Gerry And the Pacemakers. The rest of his body was like stone however, and his face never moved.   Only the fingers showed any signs of life.

Mitchell's Mercedes was of a deep brown colour.   Brown seemed to be the colour of the moment.   He had specifically requested white, but the model he had wanted had not been available in white, and he would have had to have waited three months to get it shipped.   And Mitchell was not a man to spend his time waiting for anything.   So, brown it had had to be.   Ah well, it was just a colour…

Lee Mitchell was forty-five years old.   His body was hard and powerful, though it had begun to soften around the waist, which was an obvious sign of the years advancing.   His once thick, curly black hair had thinned considerably, and had turned grey at the temples.   A combover spread over the top of his head failed to hide the fact that he had lost a lot of his hair.   But the eyes remained hard. Steely.   Never missing a detail.   His skin had retained the glow that he had always had since his youth.   Apart from his hair and stomach, he retained a youthful vigour that he knew some of his colleagues deeply envied in him.   That pleased him.   He liked people to envy him, it made him feel good about himself.   And he always did feel good about himself. He found himself briefly lost in his memories, lost in his schooldays. Moonie Mitchell. That was what they all called him, as a reference to his bright, clear skin. And even then, everyone around him envied him. Whenever he entered the room, everyone noticed, as if Rudolph Valentino had just entered the room. He had dated many girls as a young man. Some of them had even remarked upon his similarity to Valentino. Mitchell briefly glanced at himself in the rear-view mirror. Well, not so much anymore. But a bit of it was still there. He had heard many people tell him he had the matinee idol good looks and could have had a future on stage, or even in film. He appreciated the compliments, but never for one moment did he believe that that was where his future lay. Nice idea, though. Dream on, boy. Dream on.

Moonie Mitchell. It had been a long time since anyone had called him that...

Mitchell's whole life had been the building trade. His old man had been a builder but had never made it past the sites. He was dead at 65, with a dodgy back, pain in most parts of his body, and not much to show for it. A fate that

Mitchell had been determined to avoid. He had started shimmying up and down scaffolding, where his superb physique had been a huge advantage, as far back as his teens. He quickly moved upwards and onwards though to where he was now.

Right at the top.

Director of the most powerful building firm in the country.

And he was legit. Well, almost. There were still those few deals. And they were still being swept up... And blood had been spilt getting there. Some of the opposition had been forced to back down. Others had had to disappear. But building had always been a grab bag where palms had been greased, and that was understood. But sweeping up was always necessary.

Mitchell checked his watch. Three twenty-nine. In one minute, Jimmy Jarrett would be arriving. He would drive through that partition precisely at three thirty. He never failed to arrive on the dot. You could set Big Ben to him. How he achieved this, Mitchell never figured out. He had a suspicion that he always arrived fifteen minutes ahead of time, waited out of sight for fifteen minutes, and then arrived on the dot. It was a peculiar form of narcissism on Jarrett's part. The man was like a metronome. That frightened people. Every move he made felt like it had been worked out in advance. Even Mitchell was slightly afraid of him, the only man in the world he would admit to being afraid of. There were times when Mitchell had looked deep into his eyes and seen absolutely nothing there. In everyone's eyes you could read something, even if they were trying to hide it from you. But not Jarrett.

It was three thirty. Almost like a chime on a cuckoo clock, Jarrett's harvest gold MGB swept into the car park and pulled up alongside Mitchell's Mercedes. Mitchell wanted to smile but could not. It should have been amusing but because it was Jarrett, it was not.

Jarrett stepped out of the car and closed the door, looking all around as he did so. That was another thing Mitchell had noticed – Jarrett was always looking around him, checking. You could be in the middle of saying something to him and suddenly notice that he was looking all around him. Then he would refocus on you, but he had not missed a thing of what you had been telling him. He could listen and watch simultaneously. Most people could only do one thing or the other with their full attention. The driver's window was open, and Jarrett leaned in. At that moment, the bright, hopeful, eagerly optimistic sounds of the early Beatles were blasting out of the little radio. Jarrett's nostrils twitched as though he was detecting an unpleasant smell.

"That's a bit old, isn't it?" he murmured.

"I like it. And it's real music. You don't hear much of that anymore."

"Well, whatever turns you on..."

Jarrett opened the car door and eased himself into the front seat. He closed it very gently and looked at Mitchell in the rear-view mirror. Mitchell returned his gaze and found himself almost hypnotised by the black, opaque pools that were his eyes. As always, he could detect nothing in them. Mitchell was perhaps one of only two or three people who knew anything of Jarrett's history. He had been part of Operation Banner in Northern Ireland and had served with the British Army during the Troubles. He never talked about what he had done or seen during those times. He had been thrown out of the British Army during that period for reasons which had never been put on

53

record.   There had been rumours of civilian torture.   Jarrett had always maintained his innocence, but the British Army had in its wisdom decided that someone needed to be made an example of. Whatever truth there were in the rumours, and Mitchell had heard most of them, he could believe Jarrett capable of the worst of them.   Jarrett looked quite different now to how he had looked then; back then, he had been clean-shaven with close-cropped hair, indistinguishable from dozens of other squaddies.   Now the lank, black hair hung messily around his ears and crawled past the collar of his luxurious, full length black leather jacket. Like Mitchell, he was quickly balding on top.   Long, luxurious sideburns crept down to his chin.

"So, have you found my wife yet?" Mitchell asked him.   "Have you found Anna?"

"Well, there's good and bad news," Jarrett replied quietly.

Mitchell shifted slightly in his seat. "Alright, let's have it."

Jarrett's eyes bored into his.

"Mellor found her."

"Where is she?"

"A little fishing village in Devon –
Denby."

"Fishing village?"

"Right."

"I'm assuming that the bad news is
still to come…"

"Yeah. Mellor made a mistake."

"What sort of mistake?"

"It appears that he got mixed up in
a fight with one of the locals down there."

"What?"

"A right hard case, apparently.
Broke Mellor's wrist. Snapped it like a
twig. Mellor had Hollis with him. Hollis
had to go to A&E. Mellor tried to pass it
all off as a car accident. I had to hurt him
a little to get the real story."

At this Jarrett looked hard at
Mitchell. Mellor and Hollis were not part
of his organisation, but they had been
working for Mitchell. The last thing he
needed   was   the   police   asking
embarrassing questions that might lead to
him. Mitchell did not like his "people"
being manhandled, but Jarrett was his
prime asset in this case and Jarrett
assumed that he would overlook this as a
necessary judgement call. Mitchell
nodded after a few seconds.

"Sounds reasonable. What the hell was he doing mixing it with some local when he should have been after the girl?"

"The girl recognised him. Mellor then tried to frighten her into coming back with him. And that's when this stranger turned up. Apparently, he embarrassed him in front of the girl. The next morning, Mellor and Hollis tried to settle a score with him. And he made a right mess of them."

"No-one makes a mess of my people." Mitchell lit another cigarette and looked out across the urban waste ground. "You go down there, Jimmy. Take three other lads with you. Find Anna. Then make her tell you who this stranger is. I want him hurt, understand? Badly. Then bring Anna back."

Jarrett considered this as though it was a rainy day and Mitchell was suggesting that he take an umbrella with him.

"Yeah, alright," was his only reply. "Anything else?"

"No, that's all."

Jarrett should have got out of the car at that moment, but he waited for a few more beats.

"Can you imagine a sports centre standing on this very spot where we are now?" Mitchell asked him.

Jarrett shifted round in his seat and looked at Mitchell directly. "You can't deny the existence of Hell," he said softly, "but you can always build on it."

With that, Jarrett was out of the car, opening the door of his MGB, firing the engine, and roaring out of the car park.

Remy De Sica stood in the dusty gloom of the shed, looking out of the window. He had watched the whole meeting with a scowl of discomfort and displeasure on his face. Then Jarrett had gotten into his car and driven away. Remy emerged from the shed and saw the tail end of Jarrett's MGB disappear. He spat on the ground disdainfully and walked back to the Mercedes. He got into the driving seat and looked hard at Mitchell in the rear-view mirror.

"Well?"

"It's on," replied Mitchell.

"Why not let me take care of it? I can do it," Remy complained.

Mitchell looked at him levelly in the mirror. "Because I want Jarrett to do it.

Alright?"

"But Jarrett's a headcase."

"Remy," Mitchell spoke like a school-teacher addressing a disruptive pupil, "you could learn from Jarrett. Remember that. You're a bright lad, but you're not in Jarrett's league. Not yet anyway."

Remy tutted and shook his head. He was a swarthy Italian with a thick London accent, and an impeccably stylish dresser. His suits were expensive and his aftershave intoxicating. His gelled hair was combed back in the style of the mobsters from the movies. Remy wanted to be top dog. And he could bark the loudest. He had worked his way up from the back streets to become Mitchell's personal minder. And he enjoyed his work.

Mitchell exhaled. "I'm hungry. Let's get out of here."

Remy started the car and drove them out of the parking area. Halfway down the road, Mitchell's car phone trilled, and he picked it up. In the front, Remy concentrated on the road, but his ears picked up everything.

"Mitchell speaking. Oh yes… What did you say?"

Remy indicated and turned right down a residential street.

Mitchell continued in a sharper tone. "Well, tell those bastards to get a move on! I want that outfit ready to begin work in the next couple of days. And if they can't manage it, I'll lay the whole bloody lot of them off and they can try their luck down at the labour exchange. We're paying those idiots enough so they can start damn well earning it!"

There was a pause as the person on the other line tried to make up for lost ground. Mitchell stared hard through the windscreen. Finally, he spoke again.

"Tristan Head's made a bid for it? Look, I'm not worried about Tristan Head, he's not in the running anymore. You understand?" Another pause. "Look, you just make sure that site's up and moving in two days – otherwise you're up and moving. Moving out. Do you understand? *Can* you understand?" Another pause. "Then just get on with it!"

Mitchell cut the call off and slammed the phone down.

"Lemon," he spat disdainfully. He caught Remy's eyes looking at him in the rear-view mirror. "What are you looking at?" Mitchell barked. "Bloody drive!"

Remy turned his gaze away and pressed his foot on the accelerator.

It was evening by the time Mitchell arrived back at his home in Hampstead, a seven bedroom double fronted, ambassadorial style detached residence, which was grand and obscene in equal measure. The Mercedes pulled up. Remy lazily got out and opened the back door for Mitchell. Mitchell stepped out and gave Remy a disdainful glance. He pointed to his tie.

"Put your tie straight!" he ordered him. "Come on, Remy, sort yourself out." Remy shrugged and adjusted his tie.

The front door opened and a stunningly beautiful, American blond, five foot eleven, with extravagant hair, came dancing down the steps to meet Mitchell. Mitchell turned to her, smiling, with his arms out.

"Lindsay – sweetheart!"

"Hi baby!" she cooed, throwing her arms around him. She turned momentarily to glance at Remy, who made a kissing gesture with his mouth. Her smile vanished in that moment and she stared daggers at him. She mouthed a filthy epithet at him, then suddenly turned back to Mitchell and was all smiles again. She began to lead him up the steps and into the house, pulling him in. She disappeared inside.

Mitchell turned once more to Remy, ordered him away with one flick of the wrist, then the door was shut and Remy's working day was over. He looked over the huge house. One day, he thought. *One day...*

Then he got back into the car and started it up. The car crunched back down the drive and was away.

<u>6</u>

Noonan opened the door of the charity shop at the corner of the high street and stepped inside. He had spotted the place the previous evening. The door clicked softly behind him. The shop was small and cluttered but felt warm and embracing. There was no-one behind the counter, but a girl's voice called out to him.

"Be with you in a minute."

Noonan smiled as he looked around. A moment later Noonan got his first real surprise of the day. Stepping out from behind a partition was Anna. She was wearing a pair of spectacles and her auburn hair was tied back. She was wearing the same grey sweater she had been wearing the previous evening, but she now wore a knee-high black skirt and a pair of brown leather boots. It seemed entirely the wrong environment for her, but she looked settled. She clasped her fingers together and then stood to attention in the classic "can-I-help-you,

Sir?" stance adopted by many shop workers. Noonan smiled in recognition, but the girl appeared not to recognise him in return.

"I've ah..."

Still Anna continued to smile at him quizzically. Noonan glanced around the shop.

"I've come to buy some clothes. I can donate these if you want them. Or you can just throw them away..."

As he said this, Anna's professional smile became a warm and personal one.

"I'm sorry, I didn't recognise you," she said simply. "You look so different."

Noonan paused. He suddenly remembered he had had his hair cut and his beard shaved.

"Were you looking for anything in particular?" she enquired gently.

"Well, I could do with a new set of everything."

Twenty minutes later, Noonan had rid himself of his old clothes. He would have gladly burned them in a moment. He was now looking at himself in a long mirror. He was wearing a blue sweater and a pair of black jeans. Noonan never cared much about how he looked, but he was pleased with what he saw in the mirror.   At that moment Anna appeared behind him carrying a blue naval overcoat

"Try that."   She draped it over his shoulders.   Noonan looked at himself and nodded.   The overcoat was such a dark blue that it could have been black in colour. It gave him a dark, mysterious look.

"I like it," he told her.

Noonan paid for his new clothes. The bundle was absurdly cheap and at first Noonan thought that Anna had made a mistake, but she was adamant that she had not.   He kept his new clothes on, and she piled his old ones up into a brown paper bag.   He walked to the door and opened it, turning to her one last time.

"Our other two friends – I don't think you'll be seeing them.   I persuaded them it would be in their best interests to move on."

She smiled again. "Thank you."

He walked quickly through the door and was gone.   He considered Anna once again and the pang of pleasure he had felt when he had seen her in the shop.   Ever since that first meeting, he had subconsciously hoped that he would meet her again.

This was now his third day in Denby.   Earlier in the day Noonan had seen a wayfarer dinghy that had been going for sale in the harbour. It was a Mark I model, made entirely of wood, from the late 1950s, that had passed through several owners and was now going for a very reasonable £200.00. Noonan had learned how to sail a wayfarer in his late teens, the same model as the one which was currently for sale. His uncle Dennis, having recently retired from the Royal Navy, had bought himself one and took it out on the Solent most days. It had been one of the last summer holidays he could remember as being truly special. For four weeks in July, he had stayed with Dennis in Lymington. They had been out every day in the boat, often until 9pm when darkness finally fell, and it was time to go back to the harbour. During those four weeks, Dennis had taught him everything he needed to know about handling a wayfarer. The moment he had seen the dinghy, Noonan had slipped back seventeen years to that magical summer and was once again smelling the salty air and remembering the chill of the water as he had dipped his fingers over the side, the incessant squawking of the gulls around the harbour, the bittersweet taste of lemonade shandy... Dennis had died the following year of heart disease and Noonan was never destined to sail with him again. He had been as close to heartbreak at that point in his life as he had ever been, and Noonan's life afterwards had gone in a vastly different direction.

There had been a telephone number on the advertisement, which Noonan had committed to memory. He jogged back to the main high street and to the bright red telephone kiosk that he had seen several times now and put the call in. A lady's voice had answered, warm, friendly. Noonan immediately expressed interest in the boat. "Oh, it's my husband you'll be wanting to speak to – hang on, I'll just put him on...." A few seconds later, the husband's voice spoke to him down the phone, equally warm and friendly. The man introduced himself as Ralph Bellamy and was apparently delighted that the wayfarer had a potential buyer, especially as it only went on sale earlier in the week. Bellamy was happy to drive out and meet him immediately. Noonan was about to agree, then stopped himself for two reasons: firstly, he wanted to look the part for Mr Bellamy, and secondly, and more prudently, he felt that if he left it for an hour or so, he could ruminate on his decision while still having first refusal from Mr Bellamy. Noonan expressed regret that he could not be available immediately but would two hours from now work? Certainly, Bellamy assured him, that would work fine. Two thirty? Very good. They agreed to meet at the boat. Noonan could almost feel Bellamy smiling at him down the telephone, such was the warmth and ebullience that came across in his voice. Well, he had his clothes now and still had an hour to kill. He decided to sit on a bench and watch the boats.

He was still there at two thirty. He was pleased with the new clothes and felt good. Mr Bellamy arrived a minute later. Noonan knew instinctively it was him when he saw him get out of his Mini. He had a large frame, a navy blazer, and a thick handlebar moustache. He was every inch the old seadog.

Half an hour later they were out on the water. Noonan had asked to give the dinghy a trial run and Mr Bellamy had insisted that he should. It had been a long time since Noonan had worked on a wayfarer and he wanted Mr Bellamy there to function as a safety valve in case anything went wrong. The jib and the main sail went up and they were off, the wind locking onto the sail and driving the small dinghy out to sea. Noonan and Bellamy spent an exhilarating hour out on the water before coming back into harbour, at which point Noonan proclaimed that he was delighted and gladly handed over the £200.00 in cash. Mr Bellamy had been expecting a cheque and seemed a little put out that the transaction was in cash. But he quickly shrugged and accepted the money. He even threw in an outboard motor for no extra charge and helped fix it to the rear of the boat.

Noonan went straight back to the inn. There was a small garden just round the back of the inn which could be accessed through a small gate. As he was passing, something curious happened. The landlady who had been working at a hedge with a pair of shears, suddenly walked urgently towards him.

"Excuse me," she hailed him.

Noonan turned, surprised.

"Oh," she said, suddenly looking flustered, "yes, I thought it was you." She seemed embarrassed but there was a look in her eyes that Noonan had recognised many times in his life. In her eyes he could detect fear. She did not need to say anything more, her eyes communicated everything. Noonan opened the gate and walked into the garden, putting his arm around the landlady's shoulder. Instinctively he pulled her into a small nook round the side of the building away from any doors and windows. Noonan quickly looked up and around to make sure that they were neither visible nor within earshot. She did not seem to mind him touching her.

"What is it?" he asked her softly.

Her eyes did not blink when she spoke.

"There are men looking for you. They arrived two hours ago. They described you and asked if you had one of the rooms."

"How many men?"

"Four. I'm sorry, I'm afraid I told them you were staying with me."

"Don't worry about that. Where are these men now?"

"They're inside, waiting at the bar. Waiting for you, I think. I came out here to see if I could catch you before you went inside."

"What did they say?"

"Just that they were friends of yours and wanted to catch up with you —

well, I knew they were lying. I've been running this place for long enough. You get an instinct for people. And I just know there's something wrong about these people."

She paused and took a breath.

"You're not in any kind of trouble, are you? What have you been up to?"

"No, I'm not in any trouble. But I think I know who might be."

"The one who spoke to me, the leader – he had a look in his eye, I can't quite describe it, but it really frightened me."

Noonan gently let her go.

"Thank you for letting me know. Would you help me again?"

"What do you want me to do?"

"You won't be in any danger, I assure you. Now here's what I need you to do..."

7

The four men sat in the bar area. Three of the men were young and thuggish, their faces twisted into snarls of boredom. They had been sitting there for an hour and they were starting to fidget, getting on each other's nerves. They were not used to sitting and waiting. The fourth man was Jarrett. He sat like a statue with a spring tightly coiled inside him. He just stared ahead of him at the wall. Jarrett, unlike his young subordinates, had plenty of experience of waiting and it never bothered him. He had had to wait for three days on one assignment when he was in Northern Ireland. It was the coldest night of that winter and he was alone. The temperature was five below freezing, his fingers were numb and his toes in pain. Nonetheless he had waited and had thought nothing of it. He had had a job to do. An informer had given them the favoured location of a sniper working for the Provos, at the top of a disused water tower.   On the fourth morning there had been the distant clang of a door being opened below, followed by the steady shuffle of feet.   Then the donkey-jacketed shape had emerged from the shadows and moved slowly forward to his vantage point. Jarrett could make out the rifle in its case slung around his shoulder and the woolly hat on the thick head.   Then Jarrett had crept silently out from his hiding place, his hunting knife clasped in his hand.   The sniper never heard a thing, never knew what was coming.   Jarrett clamped his left hand over the sniper's mouth and cut him from ear to ear.   The warm, thick blood oozed over his fingers, the only warmth he had felt for three days. Job done. Another dead sniper.   And Jarrett's reputation as the silent menace who never failed at any job became increasingly assured.   The three lads he had taken with him could never measure up.   Despite that, they were tough and accomplished.   And they could follow orders.   He could accomplish everything he needed to down here on his own, but Mitchell had wanted him to take extra hands, and he was paying.   The lads continued to move about.

"Keep still", he ordered in a soft voice.   The moving stopped.   Jarrett was the only person who they would take orders from. Even they found him to be quietly terrifying. There was suddenly the pungent smell of burning in the air. This was followed by smoke circulating. One of the thugs started to cough. A moment later the landlady opened the door. She was wearing oven gloves and waving a hand over her face.

"I'm sorry gentlemen, I'm going to have to ask you to step out for a moment. There's been a small fire in the kitchen and we just need to clear the building. I can call you back in a few moments." The three thugs turned to Jarrett. Jarrett nodded and made a gesture towards the door with his head. They all stood up and moved towards it.

"Won't be long," called the landlady to the departing figures. Then the door was closed, and they were gone.

Outside in the street, Jarrett and the three thugs congregated. From his position in a café across the street, Noonan was able to see all of them. He was seated at a table in the centre of the room, not too near the window. From outside the building, Noonan would not be too visible. The three thugs, all furtive glances and scowls were speaking quietly amongst themselves. The leader – Noonan assumed he was the leader simply because he looked as though he was – was in a different category altogether. He was staring straight ahead of him, straight through the window into the café. Straight – it seemed – at Noonan. Had the leader spotted him? It did not seem possible. Noonan tried to read something in his expression. Idle curiosity? Recognition? Or was he just staring into the middle distance? Noonan looked down again and stared at the table. He stayed like that for two minutes. When he looked up, the four men were nowhere to be seen.

Noonan was across the road and back in the inn garden in less than a minute. He looked up. The landing window was open, just as he had instructed the landlady to leave it. There was a black drainpipe running up the side of the building. Noonan grabbed the pipe with both hands and started to climb up. He was able to climb in through the landing window without too much trouble. The landlady was waiting for him. She was pressed against the wall.

"Thanks," Noonan said. "Just give me a moment and I'll get my bag, give you my key and settle up with you, alright?"

"Alright," she replied.

Noonan moved quickly to his room. He emerged seconds later with his bag and clutching some notes in his fist. These he handed to the landlady.

"Hey, you don't owe me all this."

"I think I do." He moved back to the window, turning one last time. "Thanks. It's a lovely place you've got here. Sorry I couldn't stay longer."

"So am I," replied the landlady. Just as she started to go through the extraordinary events of the day in her mind for the first time, Noonan disappeared through the window and out of her life forever.

The bell on the door gave a 'ting' and Noonan walked hurriedly into Anna's shop. A mother and daughter brushed past him as they made their way out. Anna was behind the counter. She looked up at him and smiled vaguely. Then she saw the expression on his face.

"What's wrong?" she asked.

"You need to leave here now," Noonan told her. "There are four men here who are looking for us. I've seen them. These men are different to the other two. These men would kill you."

Noonan's eyes glittered fiercely.

"But I can't just leave right now, I've got all this." She gestured around the shop.

"You haven't got long. They could be here any minute. You need to go now."

Anna had dreaded this moment for a long time but now it was finally here, she could not believe it was happening. There was also the mystery of the man Noonan. Why had he suddenly arrived in this place and why was he doing this for her?

"Right now?" she asked, her throat suddenly going dry.

"Right now," Noonan told her firmly. He turned away and walked to the door, his mind working through the situation. He would have to leave Denby, but he had the wayfarer now. He would sail on to the next place. The girl would have to work things out for herself. He had warned her. He could do no more. He got to the door and was about to open it and walk away for good. But then he hesitated. He felt deeply conflicted. The sight of the four men approaching from the other side of the street made his mind up for him. He turned back to her.

"Do you have a back way out of here?"

"Why?"

"Because they're here."

Anna came forward and looked.

"Oh, my God." She raced back to the till, grabbed a key, rushed back, and locked the door.

"Get out through the back and wait for me – go now!" Noonan ordered.

Anna ran through an open door behind the till. The four men were now right outside the door. Jarrett tried the handle. The door rattled but did not open. Noonan looked into the black holes of Jarrett's eyes.

"Open the door," he called from the other side.

Noonan turned the 'open' sign, so it now read 'closed'. Jarrett shook his head at him. Noonan pulled the blind down, blocking out the horrible face. He walked swiftly through the back door, through a storeroom and past a lavatory. Anna was waiting outside in a courtyard.

They hurried out of the courtyard. There was a gate at the back and Noonan hustled Anna through it. He kept his arm on her as they hurried along an alleyway that led back into the town.

The alleyway ended and they ran onto the main road. Noonan immediately halted. The three thugs surrounded them. The one in the middle moved in close, a childish grin on his face.

""So where are you two going in such a hurry? We only wanted to talk to you!"

Anna clutched Noonan's arm.

"Stay behind me," he told her. The thug took a couple of steps towards Noonan.

"Back to the shop," he ordered him. "Right now." He was wearing a thick black leather jacket and a porkpie hat. His face was chubby, and he had thick triangular sideburns reaching in towards the centre of his face. He put his hand in his pocket and moved it around. "Don't make me take this out. You wouldn't want me to do that."

Noonan looked around him. Two young local boys, barely out of their teens, were sitting on a wall, casually watching. The chubby thug smirked. Noonan raised his hands in surrender and shook his head. In the next instant, his arm had shot out, his fingers balled into a fist. There was the sickening crunch of cracking bone and the chubby thug's body crashed to the tarmac, blood gushing out of his nostrils. His eyes stared wildly up at the sky, not seeing anything. He tried to get to his feet, but Noonan shot forward and kicked him once, viciously, square in the solar plexus. The thug crashed noisily back to the ground. This time, his hand went to his throat and he retched.

"Get the bastard!" he whimpered in agony. Noonan turned to face the other two, who gave each other a look and moved towards him. He predicted that they would come at him from opposite sides. It was the obvious move and Noonan was prepared for it. Both thugs charged at him from both sides. Noonan leapt into the air, his foot smashing into the groin of the thug on his right. The thug let out a howl of agony and fell to his knees. From that position he was unable to move. Noonan now focussed his attention on the last thug, who grabbed him from behind. Noonan clamped his arms behind the thug's head and pulled forward, bending his knees as he did so. The thug's body somersaulted through the air, crashing down on top of the chubby one. Noonan straightened up. The thug was scrambling to his feet.   Noonan flattened his fingers together to form a sharp edge. He bent down and smashed his flattened hand down hard behind the thug's ear. His body dropped to the ground and lay sprawled on top of his chubby mate.

Noonan straightened up.   The two boys on the wall turned and ran away.   He looked at Anna.

"Come on," he said urgently.

Anna opened her mouth, but no words came out.   He grabbed her hand again and pulled her away from the scene.

It took five minutes to get Anna down to the harbour.   There were more people there now and Noonan was able to blend in.   He needed to move quickly.   The two boys who had witnessed the fight would be reporting the incident.   But where was the fourth man?

Noonan took Anna out onto the jetty and quickly found his wayfarer.

"This is yours?" she asked.

"Yes," Noonan replied.   "And we're getting out of here on it!"

He picked up the heavy outboard motor, but just then Anna grabbed his arm and shook it.

"What is it?" Noonan snapped. Then he turned and followed Anna's gaze back to the seafront wall. Standing on the wall, staring coldly out at them, was the leader, the man Noonan had seen outside the inn. He started walking fast along it, cutting through the breeze like a phantom, the wind from the water whipping at the tails of his long, black overcoat. He never took his eyes off them. Noonan, himself unable to take his eyes off the man, started to rip at the cord on the outboard motor. It spluttered briefly and then died.

8

Anna jumped out of the wayfarer and untied it from its moorings. Noonan kept ripping at the cord, but the engine would not catch.

"Come on!" he shouted in desperation. Anna got back into the boat and grabbed at the cord also.

Noonan looked up and could see that the man was nearly upon them. He had jumped off the wall and onto the jetty and was now running at full speed towards them. There were a couple of seamen there. The man shoved past them, nearly knocking one of them into the water.

"Hey! Watch where you're going – idiot!" he called after him furiously. The man's expression was a mask of concentration and deadly intent. All the time he seemed to be gathering speed.

The engine coughed and died. It was no good! Noonan cursed Mr Bellamy and the faulty outboard motor he had left him with.

The man's foot slammed down on the edge of the jetty and he leapt with a thunderous crash into Noonan's boat, causing it to swing dangerously from side to side.

Anna let out a scream, but Noonan was already bringing up an oar that was lying at his feet. He tried to shove it into the man's throat, but he was far too late. The man tore it out of Noonan's hands, then viciously head-butted him. Noonan fell backwards into the boat. Then the man was on top of him and forcing the oar down onto his throat. Noonan could feel himself fighting for breath. He gripped the oar with both hands and tried to force it away, using all the strength that he had. But the oar just kept pushing harder into his throat...

Then suddenly the oar came away and the man was stumbling around in the boat, rubbing the side of his head, a look of pain and bewilderment on his face. Anna was standing behind him with a second oar raised in the air. She brought it down hard again on the man's temple. He dropped the oar, turned, and smacked Anna hard across the face as though swatting away an irritating wasp. Anna fell back against the side of the boat. The man was then coming back at Noonan, but Anna's intervention had given him time to get to his feet. He threw himself at the man, his fist raised, aiming for his throat. But the man's arms came quickly up, grabbing Noonan's arm and twisting. Noonan yelled out in pain. It was as though he was fighting himself in a mirror. The man seemed able to read his thoughts ahead of time. Noonan was forced slowly down onto his knees. Noonan grabbed the oar with his left hand, lifted it and brought it heavily down on the man's head. The man yelled out in pain, releasing him. Noonan grabbed him by the coat and pulled him down. Then the two of them were rolling around on the floor of the boat. Noonan got on top of the man, his hands around his throat. He squeezed, using every ounce of strength left in him, his face contorted in desperation. The man kicked out at Noonan's stomach, propelling Noonan's body backwards.

The man tried to leap up after him, but Noonan grabbed his leg, lifting it higher and higher into the air. The man hopped backwards on his other leg, swinging his arms uselessly. Noonan pushed the man forward furiously. The man fell against the edge of the boat.

Noonan gave one last push to throw him overboard, but the man had jack-knifed forward and managed to grab Noonan's coat. But then Anna came between them, bringing her oar down hard on the man's arms. He let out a cry and released his grip on Noonan. Seizing his chance, Noonan grabbed the man's ankle and lifted. His body flipped upwards, and over the side, hitting the water with an enormous splash. Noonan felt the water hitting him in the face. The man's body momentarily disappeared under the surface.

"The motor!" Noonan shouted at Anna, but she was already there, pulling away at the cord. The motor growled and died. Anna pulled again, yanking the cord, and running backwards with it. The motor roared into life. The man's face broke the surface of the water then, and he started swimming towards the boat. Noonan grabbed the oar and hit out hard at the man's bobbing head, smashing it into his teeth. Blood oozed out of his mouth. The man grabbed the oar and pulled. But then the dinghy was surging forward and away, cutting through the water. Noonan could see the man uselessly holding the oar up into the air.

Then he let it fall into the water, his head, disappearing into the distance, bobbing up and down like a lost buoy. The man opened his mouth and let out a blood-curdling scream of fury that chased them with the wind out of the harbour. And then his head dipped under the water and was gone.

Noonan ran to the back of the boat and grabbed the rudder, steering the boat away from the harbour and into the channel until it was alone. Anna crouched down at the side of the boat, grabbing the edge with both hands. The wind whipped at her strawberry blond hair. She turned, looking pale and shaken. Their eyes met and held each other for a moment. Noonan turned the motor off. The engine spluttered, coughed and then went silent. The dinghy bobbed sleepily in the water. Noonan stepped over to Anna and sank down beside her, exhausted. His arm throbbed, his throat ached, and he felt dizzy. They sat there together for a while, neither of them saying anything, both feeling physically and emotionally drained.

Noonan looked at her grey sweater and black skirt and realised that they would provide scant protection from the chilly winds that would blow in from the channel later in the day. Immediately he took his naval overcoat off and offered it to her.

"Here," he said softly.

She let him drape the coat around her shoulders. He examined the mark on her cheek.

"It's just a bruise, nothing serious. Are you OK?"

Anna nodded once. "I think so." She turned and looked at him directly. "Thank you."

He smiled quickly. He then looked up at the sails.

"The first thing we need to do is get this boat moving. Have you ever sailed before?"

"No."

"Well, this is a wayfarer and needs two people to work it. There's a main sail and a smaller one, called the jib. I'm going to need you on the jib. OK?"

She nodded. "OK."

Noonan stood up and unravelled the main sail and the jib. He hooked the main sail to the mast and heaved it up to the top. The jib was, as Noonan had indicated, much smaller in size and fitted to the other side of the mast.

"One important thing to remember is that when we change direction, the sail is going to swing around fast and if you don't keep your head down, it could hit you hard. If you hear me shout, "ready about – *lee-ho!*", you just remember to duck. OK?"

She was staring at him distantly and did not immediately reply.

"Look Anna, I know you've had a shock, but I need you to focus right now. Alright?" Noonan snapped. "You have to help me sail this thing."

"I've got it," she replied quietly. She was looking at him vacantly, only half-hearing what he was telling her. He seemed to be recovering quickly from the assault while she was still shaking inside.

"I'll be on the rudder and the main sail. Now we just need the wind…"

At that moment, as if it had been waiting for its cue, the main sail locked into position and the wind thrust the little dinghy forward hard. Noonan grabbed the rudder with his left hand and steered the little dinghy ahead. He kept the main sail held taut in his right hand. "Just grab that rope in front of you for me and hold it tight." She did so. "That's it. And if I tell you to let it out, just let it out a bit."

Anna nodded. She looked out across the horizon, unable to get the ghastly image of the man who had attacked her out of her mind. She shuddered at the memory of his face. But then she turned to face the man who had been there for her and she immediately began to feel better. She had rarely had the chance to sail, but there was something about the speed of the boat zipping through the water, the wind crashing in her ears, and the water rising and falling all around her that she found both romantic and intoxicating. The next hour was just the two of them working the boat together and soaring through the waters. He barked instructions at her and she obeyed. Amazingly, the nightmare of the man who had chased them seemed to ebb away. She had started to become caught up in the thrill of the moment with the enigmatic stranger. There was no doubt in her mind who had sent the men. But should she tell this man everything as soon as an opportunity presented itself? No, better not. If he understood how serious her troubles were, he may decide to abandon her and move on without her. She would not blame him. These were her problems, after all, not his. But there was something tremendously exciting about being on the boat with him. She quickly realised that she very much wanted to stay with him, the stranger with the eyes of an angel and the heart of a hunter and hoped that she would.

"Ready about!", he called over to her. *"Lee-ho!"*

Anna quickly ducked and the main sail swung viciously round and locked into position. The boat swung around to starboard. Anna could imagine the pain of being hit by the heavy sail.

They blasted their way through the rolling waters. There were only a couple of other boats out on the horizon and, beyond them, the hint of grey clouds rolling in. And then the dreadful memory of the man's face flared up again in Anna's mind. She feared deeply that she would see it again. Her cheek still stung from where he had smacked her earlier.

"That man," she called out to Noonan. "He's going to come after us again, isn't he?"

"Yes," nodded Noonan. "So, we'll just have to be cleverer than him and stay one step ahead."

She nodded.

"What brought you to Denby?"

"I just happened to be in the area."

"Why?"

"Well, I have to be somewhere, I guess."

"Where were you before then?"

He shrugged. "Somewhere else."

"Well, that tells me a lot," she replied, a hint of a smile on her face for the first time. "Is that what you've been doing all this time? Just moving from place to place?"

"That's what most people do. Maybe you've been doing it too. Let the jib out a little there." She did so. "Look, Anna. It doesn't take a lot to see that you're in serious trouble, judging from the men back there." He looked out across the horizon. "Well, I know a bit about that myself."

"You're in trouble too?"

"Yes. And one day – maybe – we'll tell each other all about it."

9

The landlady of the inn wiped the surface of the bar area with a damp cloth. The surface was sticky with the spilt beer and ring marks from the glasses that had been used the previous evening. She pushed the cloth along, feeling it cut through the stickiness until the surface was as shiny as a mirror. The memory of the events of the morning were still very much troubling her. She had spent the last two hours telling herself that it had all worked out for the best and that she had acted nobly, bravely. Nonetheless, there had been the voice inside her telling her that she would have been better to have left well alone. She was still conflicted in her mind. But she had been afraid for the stranger with the kind eyes and could not have turned a blind eye to the danger he had surely been in. Then there had been the other man, the man with the terrifying eyes, black eyes that had held no emotion, two bottomless pits of emptiness. Well, he was gone too. What had her houseguest been through? She shrugged the question away. There would never be an answer to that question and perhaps she did not want to know in any case.

She walked back into the kitchen. And froze. She could feel the blood draining from her face. Standing facing her was the man with the black eyes. He was standing a few feet inside the kitchen from the open door to the garden. The threat of terrible danger seemed to throb from the man, and she could feel it. There was a nasty red gash across his mouth, and it looked as if someone had carelessly applied lipstick across his swollen mouth, which was twisted into a ghastly grimace. The whites of his eyes seemed to shine out at her across the room.

"I'm sorry, you're not supposed to be here," she heard herself saying to him. She tried to load as much authority into her voice as she could. Nonetheless, she could hear her voice shaking slightly as she said it.

The man said nothing.

"I said you're not supposed to be here!" the landlady repeated to him, hardening her voice. "This part of the premises is private! I think you'd better get out!"

The man did not move.

"Now!" barked the landlady, now really feeling the hopelessness of her situation.

"The door was open."

The man's voice was reedy, like the whisper of a serpent. It brought a chill to the room. His eyes held hers like the black barrels of two revolvers. She then noticed something extremely odd about the man. He was soaking wet. Water was dripping from his thick, ankle-length black leather overcoat. Two small puddles were forming on the linolineum on the floor. Sopping streaks of his jet-black hair hung down his face like frayed lengths of string. His trousers and black shirt clung to him, giving him the appearance of a scarecrow. His face had a white pallor, and his cheekbones had the sharp, razor-like edges of a rock face.

"What do you want here?" The landlady's voice had started to falter, and she could sense him picking up on this.

"Who else is here? Right now?" His voice slithered across the room at her.

"Well, there's Janet, who's upstairs changing the sheets...."

"Janet."

The man spoke the name in a dull monotone. He seemed to be processing the name. Finally, he nodded once.

"Are you married?" He asked.

For a moment she forgot her fear of the man and felt angry. He had no right – and no reason – to be asking this. She felt affronted.

"Now what business is that of yo....?"

The landlady stopped. The man's eyes were suddenly blazing with a wild insanity and she felt a chill instantly trickle right the way down to the base of her spine.

"Are you married?" he asked again, in the same tone of voice.

"I was. My husband died two years ago. I've been running this place on my own since then."

The eyes dulled over again. There was nothing there now, no sympathy.

"I need a hot bath. And I need these clothes washed and dried. And I want it done immediately."

She nodded. She was aware of the dull, distant ticking of a nearby clock hanging over the cooker and the distant creaking of floorboards as Janet went about her business of changing the sheets in one of the rooms upstairs. The air in the room seemed to eat away at her. The man reached into the pocket of his black leather overcoat, fished around and then smiled grimly.

"Ah..." he muttered. "I seem to have lost my wallet. So, I cannot pay you. But I will tell you what I'll do – are you listening?"

"Yes."

"If you do what I want you to do, I'll forget that you warned our friend off earlier today. You had no business doing that. And frankly..." His eyes bored into hers and pointed out at her like the barrels of two revolvers. "...Why did you do that?"

"I..."

Her mouth opened again but no words came out. The man crooked his head inquisitively.

"I didn't."

"But he knew to run away. How else would he have known if you hadn't warned   him?"

"I – I was afraid..."

"That sort of thing usually makes me incredibly angry."

She nodded.

"Sit down." He ordered her. He indicated to a wooden chair in the corner of the kitchen. She found herself doing as she had been ordered. Being seated made her feel in an even more hopeless position. What happened next was utterly bewildering. The man pulled off his leather jacket and let it drop to the floor with a soft whump. Then he unbuttoned his black shirt and let this fall on top of it. He was performing a striptease for her, the unhinged glare suddenly creeping back into his eyes. She could not, dared not, look away from him. The gun barrels of the eyes were always trained on her. In a few seconds he was standing in front of her wearing just his underpants. His clothes were piled in a sodden heap at his feet. The landlady reflected that any other man who would strip himself down in her kitchen would appear ridiculous, comical. But not this man. Now he appeared before her like a wild animal. He reminded her of the stranger with the kind eyes who had just departed from her. But this man was a vastly different proposition. The landlady found her eyes rivetted to an ugly purple scar right in the middle of his chest. It seemed to cover the entire width of his chest.   The man followed her gaze and quickly looked down at his chest.

"What are you looking at?" he demanded coldly.

The landlady just shook her head and let her eyes drop to the floor.

"Where's the bathroom?" he then wanted to know.

"I'll take you," she breathed, and suddenly ran for the kitchen door, reaching out for the pearl handle.

"Hold it!"

The man's voice was high, almost screeching.   She froze and turned around, trying to appear as unfazed and irritated as she possibly could.   He moved towards her again.

"I want you to take me to his room."

"If you insist," she shrugged at him, feigning weary bemusement, "if that would make you happy."

"Go on," he ordered her.   She opened the door and moved towards the staircase.   All the time she could feel the man's shadow looming over her like a shadow cast by a gravestone.   She hurried up the stairs trying hard to escape the dreadful shadow that followed her every step of the way.   She opened the door at the top and moved quickly down the corridor towards the room at the end. At that moment one of the other doors opened and Janet hurried out carrying a set of towels. The man appeared at the door with just his underpants. Startled, Janet's eyes widened. She backed towards the door of the room she had just come out of. She felt behind her for the door handle. She grasped it, twisting, and backed quickly into the room. The door closed with a soft click. Jarrett appeared not to have noticed her at all.

"This one?" he asked the landlady. She nodded, unlocking the door. She hurried inside. She positioned herself by the bed as though she were about to give him a tour of the room. The door swung wide open and the man stood framed in the doorway. He slowly closed the door. The landlady could hear the door down the corridor click open and the soft patter of Janet's feet on the carpet as she hurried to the stairs.

The man lifted his hand and clicked his fingers. Once. Twice. Again. And again. Like a metronome. Perfectly in rhythm, terribly slow like a distant heartbeat. The black opaque eyes moved across her face like slugs. The landlady just stood there, baffled, bewildered, waiting for it to end. She emptied her mind of all thoughts. She must see this thing through. She must not let this man frighten her. She would not let this man frighten her. This was just a piece of theatre to try and upset her. She allowed her eyes to glaze over and concentrated her gaze at the centre of the man's forehead. There was a tiny spot there and she stared at it. She was not aware of how long she had stood there while the clicking continued, time just seemed to stand still. She suddenly felt very tired and sleepy. The man lowered his arm and seemed to float towards her. He stopped two feet in front of her.

"Don't leave the building. If you do, I will know."

The landlady found herself unable to move.

"But if you help me, I'll be out of here as soon as possible and you'll never see me again."

It felt like an effort, but the landlady nodded once. The man walked past her and into the bathroom. He closed the door. The landlady stood for a few moments, hearing the shower being turned on. Then she turned and hurried out of the room, the blood burning in her ears and her breath coming in and out, in and out, in short gasps.

Jarrett stood in the shower, the water tumbling around his ears. He knew little of the sensation of pleasure and did not care to pursue it for its own sake. The greatest pleasure in his world was a job completed, especially if it involved a killing. But he had to admit that the sensation of the hot water on his freezing body felt especially luxurious. The water had been cold as hell and his upper gum throbbed with a sharp, stinging pain. Jarrett pointed his mouth up to the jet of hot water and allowed the water to get at it. His feet had been feeling like lumps of ice. Now the warmth of the water brought the stinging sensation of feeling back into them. He put his damp, stringy hair under the water and rubbed soap furiously through it.

With the return of feeling to his body also came the return of the anger. The anger that would dig deep inside him whenever he had something he needed to do. The anger was kicking in now. He could see the other man's face clearly in his mind. The clear grey eyes that glittered with hardened experience and something despicable like compassion. He remembered his precise, panther-like movements on the boat. Jarrett had remembered feeling confused and rattled. The man had seemed to be able to predict every move he made and had finally beaten him. He had seen the grimace of victory in his face as he had driven the oar into his mouth. Jarrett had never been beaten before and he was still trying to understand this. The anger was throbbing up through his veins now and he was not able to control it. The palm of his hand shot out and started hammering on the tiles. Hard. Harder. Again, and again.

Bastard! Bastard! Bastard!

He would find him. And he would kill him. And he would look into his eyes as he did so. And it would feel good.

And what of the girl Anna? How did she connect with him? She had fought back on the boat, which he had not allowed for. He would not make that oversight again. For as long as they were together, they were strengthened. Well, he would just have to separate them. Permanently. And then he would take her back. And at this moment in time nothing else mattered. He had been given this job to do and he never failed on a job. But this job was going to be different. For the first time as a fringe benefit, he would be doing a special favour to himself.

All he could see in his mind in that moment was the face of the man. And he wanted to crush it.

He would see to it that it would be done.

He always did.

He lay on the bed and stared up at the ceiling. He was waiting. He had to wait. There was nothing else he could do. But he was growing impatient. Anna and the man were getting further and further away. And the trail would soon be getting cold. And he needed to get after them. But first he needed his dry clothes. His body and hair were drying nicely.

He started to curse the woman downstairs. Why was it taking her so long to dry his clothes? That stupid, bloody useless woman. He would happily have seen to her too but that would only cause him further problems later. He did not want to be in this place any longer than he had to be. He could smell the fear from the landlady. So, she should get up here and give him his clothes. Then he would be away. They would be doing each other a favour.

He was aware of the sound of the tumbler dryer being turned off downstairs. Good. Get up here, you... There was the patter of feet on the stairs, down the corridor and then the inevitable knock on the door.

"Yes!" He shouted impatiently.

She opened the door and came in with his clothes, neatly folded. She stood in front of him nervously.

"Bring them over," he murmured. She moved carefully forward, and he snatched them from her. Then he looked up at her and waved her away in a gesture of dismissal. She quickly left the room.

Jarrett stood up and started to dress himself.

He appeared in front of her five minutes later. His hair was combed straight back and clung to the back of his skull. His face was showing a little pink, having been under the hot water, but in every other respect he looked dismayingly cadaverous.

"I'm going now," he said softly and simply. He might have been a small boy talking to another small boy. The landlady tried not to look too relieved. Instead, she kept her expression fixed on her face. She said nothing but she felt her pulse quickening.

"I'm going to need some money," he then told her without any emotion. The landlady's heart began sink but then she told herself that she was nearly rid of him. This was the final hurdle. If she did give him some money, then he would hopefully leave, and she would be rid of him. At least he had told her he would leave.

She moved towards her handbag and dug into her purse. The money that Noonan had given her was there. She decided to give him all of it. The heartbreak of gaining so much money and losing it in the same day was nothing compared to the need to get rid of this man. He snatched the money and shoved it into his jacket pocket. There was no need for him to then slap her to the ground and grab her bag to see if there was any more money in there, but he did it anyway. The landlady shrieked and went down, shaking on the cold, hard floor. Satisfied that she had given him all the money, he then turned and walked out of the kitchen and out of her life forever. But the memory of this hideous man and the two hours he had spent with her would stain her forever.

Jarrett had lost his car keys as well as his wallet in the water. His gold MGB car remained in the spot where he had parked it earlier, at the bottom of the road leading up to the church. He looked casually around. No-one was around. He lifted his leather-jacketed elbow and smashed the window at the driver's seat. He unlocked the car and opened the door. Wiping the seat clean of all jagged pieces of glass, he climbed in and closed the door. He leaned over and found the wires he needed to hotwire the car. The engine roared into life and he tore off back down the road, mounting the kerb on the other side of the road as he did so.

At last, he could get moving.

He was going to pick up their trail.

He knew exactly how to do it.

10

The winds on the water were incredibly fierce that day, which was fortunate for Noonan and Anna, as wayfarers are entirely dependent on wind power to propel them forward. They had now been sailing for five hours and Noonan estimated that they must have covered around twenty-five miles in that time.

It was now half past six in the evening. The daylight was fading rapidly.

The wind velocity had dropped but it had grown considerably chillier. It blew around Anna's ears and her strawberry blond hair danced like fire in the cold evening air. She kept her arm on the jib, but it was starting to weigh heavily. A dull pain started to grow in the pit of her stomach, and she was suddenly aware that she had eaten nothing since breakfast. She looked across at the barren landscape drifting idly alongside them. There had not been a settlement for a couple of hours now. Noonan was looking out to the horizon, a troubled expression on his face. Eventually he turned to Anna.

"Who was that man, Anna?"

Anna looked at him for a moment, a hint of suspicion and fear still in her eyes but did not reply.

"Anna?"

Still no reply.

Losing patience, Noonan moved forward and grabbed both her shoulders. He squeezed gently.

"Look, Anna, you have to tell me. He's after both of us now, not just you. Do you understand? And if we're going to get through this alive, then we need to trust each other. Now who was he?"

"He works for my husband!" she then blurted out. "So did the two who came before him."

She then forcibly removed Noonan's hands from her shoulders and moved away, rubbing them gently.

"Who is he, your husband?" Noonan continued, in a softer voice.

"He's the director of one of the biggest building corporations in this country," she replied, in a quieter, more controlled tone. "He's a very dangerous man. He's had people killed."

"And now he's after you?"

She hesitated again.

"He is, isn't he?"

"Yes, he's after me."

"Why?"

"Because I found out too much about him. He came after me and I had to run away. I thought I'd be safe. I was for nine months."

"Until those two guys found you?"

She nodded again.

"Why are you helping me?" she then asked.

"Because I was there."

He turned back to the horizon and offered no further explanation. There was a pause.

"What about you?" she asked, prompting him. "What are you running from?"

She looked carefully at Noonan. His eyes glazed over, and he seemed to be getting further away from her. She was about to repeat the question but the sound of distant singing coming from the darkening shore distracted her from her thoughts. It was a mixture of adult and children's voices, singing in harmony. Noonan turned to scan the shore. He could see twenty lanterns glowing in the darkness and directed the boat towards the shore to get a closer look. The singing assembly were walking along the path, their soft, caressing voices floating along on the sea breeze, carrying Noonan and Anna along with them.

The boat came up alongside the singers. As they did so, one of the adults turned to them and raised a hand in greeting. Noonan returned the greeting. Very quickly the boat overtook the singers and drifted on into the late evening. And then the grey, milky light faded to blackness.

Noonan was suddenly aware of how cold it was. He looked at Anna and could see that she was shivering. She was crouching down in the boat hugging her knees to her stomach. He realised that neither of them had eaten for several hours now.

"There must be a village further up the channel. Those people must have been on their way somewhere," Noonan said to her. She smiled encouragingly up at him as if to reassure him, "I'm doing fine, don't worry about me."

"You're hungry," he said to her.

"I'm OK."

"When we get to the next village, we'll get some food there." In fact, he had no idea how far away the next village would be. Privately he was starting to worry. He was aware that sailing a dinghy in the darkness was extremely difficult at best and hazardous at worst. Sailing purely on visual feedback from the sails was nearly impossible. They continued to drift onwards for another two hours, by which point the darkness was complete and had swallowed them up. Noonan may as well have been sailing with his eyes shut. He could not see a thing. He peered hard at his watch. It was now half past eight. He checked around on the boat. There was a sheet of tarpaulin that they could both sleep on if necessary, though Noonan hoped it would not have to come to that. There was a lantern by his feet which – thank God – had a battery inside it. The light that it emitted was not as sharp as he would have liked but it was good enough. It cast a faint, yellow glow across the water.

Noonan was suddenly aware that the girl was standing next to him. Her tall, leonine figure stood firm against the background of the night.

"You're worried." Her eyes searched his enquiringly.

"We don't know what's along this stretch of the channel, Anna. We can't see and we can't navigate. If we hit any fierce winds..." He let the sentence hang in the chilly night air.

She let her arm rub against his and he felt the weight of her body pressing gently against him. He was suddenly less aware of the cold breeze in the air.

"You've done so much for me today – and I can't even remember your name," she said quietly.

"My name is Tom Noonan."

"That wasn't your name yesterday."

"I didn't know you then. But Tom Noonan is my real name. And if it means anything, you're the first person I've told."

"Tom Noonan," she repeated, turning the name over in her mind. "Yes, that's more like it."

"I still don't know your full name."

"Anna Raven."

He nodded. It suited her. He liked it.

"I'm trying to figure you out, Tom. I've a feeling it's going to take a while. I may never even get there."

"Well, good luck with that." He looked back at her, an amused smile on his face, and then she was smiling back at him.

They stayed like that for a few moments. Then he turned to look out into the black abyss ahead of him and the moment was gone. She turned away from him and looked towards the shore, staring out into the murky, inky void. She shivered. She could almost feel the presence of the man out there in the blackness, waiting for them to stop so that he could pounce on them like a predator. She turned to her left and looked upriver. They both saw it at the same time.

"Noonan!" she called out, raising a finger. Out of the darkness a phosphorescent orange light was glowing.

"That's it!" he called back to her. "Let's get over there."

The orange glow soon became a series of orange lights, which soon became a series of buildings. Squares of light blazed out of windows on ground floors and first floors. There came the faint, ambient sound of voices spilling out of a local pub and tumbling away into the night. An occasional guffaw split the night air followed by high laughter. The buildings grew larger and more clearly defined until they could feel themselves moving past them. Noonan directed the boat into a small harbour that jutted out into the water. Peering out into the darkness lit by his lantern, Noonan could see the end of a short, narrow jetty. There was enough room for him to moor the Wayfarer up to the end.

Noonan threw Anna the mooring rope. Smiling, she caught the rope. The boat knocked against the jetty. Anna jumped excitedly onto the side of the boat and over. She tied the rope around the mooring and waited for Noonan. He turned the lantern off, put it away, lifted his legs over and joined her on the jetty.

She was about to start walking when he gently took her arm and squeezed it. "Keep your eyes open," he told her. "He could be here. He'll know we're bound to pass through here sooner or later."

"You think he's already here?" she asked, fear creeping into her voice.

"All we can do is hope that we got here ahead of him," he replied grimly.

They walked carefully up the jetty. Noonan's eyes darted everywhere, peering into every crevasse, every square inch of blackness for something that did not belong, a movement in the shadows that could mean the very worst kind of trouble. But there was no-one. They made it to the end of the jetty and onto the road.

Noonan looked up and down the road. The tavern was over to the right with leathery-faced local men and their ladies tumbling in and out. Instinctively Noonan put his right arm around Anna's shoulders and guided her away from the tavern. They walked on the pavement, hugging the shadows. Noonan's eyes continued to look everywhere. Every black window might possibly conceal a malevolent face peering out at them. There had to be an inn around here somewhere. He just did not want to take too long to find it. Something inside him told him that he did not have long.

A man staggered along on the pavement on the other side of the street. He belched once and staggered on. Noonan and Anna came to an end and turned right around a corner. Noonan immediately saw a hotel sign glowing in the darkness with three stars emblazoned across its name: Rheda Hotel. Noonan did not take in the name of the place; it was not important. He was only glad to get there. He looked at his watch. It was half past nine. They would still be open, but they would have to hurry. He bundled Anna along the road, turned underneath the hotel sign, opened the door and hurried in.   The door closed softly behind them.

At the end of the street, a car turned in, the headlights questing through the darkness like the red eyes of a wolf. The car prowled along at low speed, its antenna probing every alley and doorway. A black, malign shape was hunched over the steering wheel, the head idly turning from right to left as the car moved.

The car passed the front door of the Rheda Hotel.   It was a golden MGB.

11

The reception area of the hotel was crepuscular and smelled of tobacco. There was a reception desk to the right of them and a white painted staircase running up to a landing with a red carpet. There was a room off to the left, which was dimly lit. Smoke lazily drifted through the open door into the reception area. A wheezy cough could be heard from the room. Noonan guessed that it was a rest or a reading room. There was a wooden desk running across the reception area and an old register with yellowing, dog-eared pages. A car drifted slowly past outside, casting shadows that wiped their way across the ceiling. There was no bell on the desk.

A shadow fell across the room and Noonan turned around. A grey-haired man with a long grey beard appeared from the rest room and shuffled into the reception area. He lifted a section of the desk and came round to face them.

"Good evening," Noonan greeted him softly. There was no response from the man. Either he had not heard him, or he had chosen not to. The grey-haired man placed the palms of his hands firmly down on the wooden surface, pressing them in. He fixed Noonan with a cold, slightly hostile stare. Noonan felt Anna shifting uncomfortably next to him. The man wore a baggy grey sweater, brown corduroy trousers and a red club tie over a white shirt that looked as though it had not seen the inside of a washing machine for a long time.

"I'm sorry for our late arrival," Noonan said to him in his most gracious voice.

The man looked at his watch. Noonan glanced up at a clock over the reception area. It was twenty-five to ten.

"You're wanting a room?" The man's voice was hard and challenging with a strong hint of the west country.

"Well, yes." Noonan started to bumble in the manner of a clueless holiday maker who was desperately trying to find his way around. "My wife and I have recently bought a boat and we thought we'd come down here and do a little sailing. Well," he stifled a laugh, "we started off from Ilfracombe and stayed out a little too long. Suddenly it was dark, and I couldn't see my own hand in front of my own face…"

Beside him Anna fixed the hotelier with a warm, bright, bubbly smile, expertly and immediately adapting herself to the role of The-clueless-holidaymaker's-equally-clueless-but-nonetheless-insufferably-jolly-wife. Her bright green eyes were radiant with apologetic cheeriness.

"Actually, it's my fault," she butted in, "I was the one who wanted to keep going. I just didn't realise how far out we'd come…" She turned to Noonan. "You were absolutely right darling; we should have turned back when you suggested."

"Oh well, it's done now," Noonan sighed with weary resignation. He turned back to the hotelier. "I know it's late, but you wouldn't have a room for the night?"

The hotelier looked from one to the other. Anna's eyes pleaded with him. The hotelier studied them with indifference. The little pantomime that they had staged for his benefit appeared to have had no effect on him. Then he spoke softly and slowly.

"The door should have been locked. We don't normally admit anyone after 9pm."

"I'm sorry for the intrusion," Noonan replied. The man continued to study them. Noonan became aware of the smell of alcohol that was emanating from the man. He was already thinking ahead to what his possibilities were if they were not to be admitted.

"You started out from Ilfracombe?" he asked Noonan with suspicion in his eyes.

Noonan had not had time to prepare a cover story. He had been wary of saying they had come from Denby. He silently worried to himself that he had made a mistake in using Ilfracombe as a starting out point. What if the man knew the area well? He may have friends there. Oh well, too late now. He would just have to face it out.

"That would take you more than a day," he told them. "I would have thought."

"We started early," Noonan replied, rather lamely in his opinion.

At that moment, a woman with iron grey hair came down the stairs. Her hair was tied back in a bun. She wore a long skirt and a navy-blue cardigan. As soon as she saw Noonan and Anna her face broke into a warm and welcoming smile. Noonan experienced a wave of relief. It was immediately obvious that this was the hotelier's wife, and she was as hospitable as he was suspicious.

"Good evening!" She beamed at them. "Will you be needing a room?"

"Oh, yes please!" replied Noonan.

"Well, all our rooms are booked but you may have our guest room."

"That's very kind of you," Anna replied, smiling at her.

The wife lifted the flap and came round the desk, delicately pushing her husband out of the way. He stepped back, still glowering at the intruders.

"Where have you come from then?"

"Bexleyheath. I was just saying we've recently bought a boat and we thought we'd try a little sailing down here." Noonan repeated the whole story all over again. He reasoned that the lady must have heard this story thousands of times over the years and had probably tuned out after the Bexleyheath revelation. If the couple had lived in this village all their lives — which was likely — Bexleyheath would have meant as much to them as a spot on the Antarctic. It would do. The husband's eyes dulled over as Noonan and Anna went into their routine. As Noonan spoke, he was looking at Anna and he was impressed. She had her role down perfectly. She had the most marvellously expressive eyes, and she knew how to use them.

"Now, would you mind signing the register?" She swivelled the old book round, opened it, and thrust it forward. She then thumped a pen down in front of them. Noonan picked it up and wrote simply, *"Mr and Mrs D Cavell, Bexleyheath."* Anna watched him write, switching on her smile again for the woman.

"Thank you. I'll show you to your room." The wife was already moving quickly up the stairs. Noonan nodded once to the hotelier who did not nod back. He moved quickly after the wife followed by Anna.

There was a narrow passageway at the top and several doors on either side. There were several nooks and crannies where other doors to other rooms were half-hidden. At the end of the corridor was a steep staircase that looked positively dangerous. The place was like a rabbit warren. There was a musty, cobwebby smell about it. It was a strange setup, but Noonan felt glad to be there. At the end on the right there were three steps leading down to a door. She took out a key and unlocked it. The room was facing the street. This was bad news, but they would have to accept it. She opened the door and turned on the light.

"Here we go then." She smiled again. The room was ridiculously small and poky with a small bed in the middle. The window looked straight out onto the street.

"You've been very kind, thank you," replied Noonan.

"Breakfast is from 7.30 onwards."

Noonan nodded and smiled. The woman backed through the door. He grabbed Anna's arm and indicated silence with his face. He listened and waited for the woman's footsteps to recede down the corridor. Soon there was silence. He released her arm. Anna started to move towards the window.

"Stay away from the window!" Noonan's voice cracked across the room like a whip. Instantly Anna stopped. She looked back at him and instantly understood. She came back to him and

pressed herself against the door. Noonan
turned the lights out. He moved carefully
to the edge of the window and peered down
into the street. Outside nothing was
moving. Noonan glanced at all the
windows across the street. Each one was
as black as a well, its secrets never to be
revealed to the night. Noonan carefully
pulled the curtains closed. He turned and
nodded to Anna, who turned the light on.
The empty room smiled back at them
innocently.

Anna moved to the bed and sat
down on it, bouncing gently. Noonan
moved about the room, inspecting every
part of it. It was about as perfunctory as
one could imagine. For a guest room one
would have to feel only sympathy for the
guests. Noonan could not imagine that
the hotelier and his wife were inundated
with friends anyway. And the room did
not feel as if it had been occupied for a long
time. It was an uncomfortable, unsettling
room. The bed was hardly big enough for
two. Not that that would be an issue
tonight. There was an armchair by the
window and Noonan would sleep in that.
He could see that the same thought was
going through Anna's mind. She lay back
on the bed.

"I wouldn't hurt you, you know," she smirked at him.

"Do you promise?"

He went to the armchair and sat, dragging his bag with him. He opened it and took out his money, counting it.

"We're running low on money," he told her. "We'll pay for the room, get some provisions tomorrow, then that's most of it gone."

"So, what do we do?"

"I have a friend. My only real friend. He might be able to help." Anna was looking at him, waiting for more information. "He sends me money whenever I need it. Leaves it at the local Post Office in whatever town I happen to be."

"For a certain Mr Cavell?"

"That's right."

"Because there's someone – or some people – out there that you're running away from."

"Yes."

There was a pause. Anna wanted to know so much more but knew it would be wrong to press the matter further. At least for the moment.

"Tell me about your friend."

"What do you want to know?"

"Well, for example, what does he do?"

"He's a millionaire, a builder, like your husband.   And he's the one man in the world I can completely trust."

"How long have you known him?"

"We were together in the army.   He was my Commanding Officer.   Yes, Tristan's always been there for me."

"Tristan?"

Anna watched him carefully. Noonan's body noticeably relaxed and he looked slightly away at the wall.   His eyes softened.   Suddenly he was years away, enjoying happy memories of happier times. The walls had come down and a note of sentiment came into his voice.

"My mate, Tristan.   Tristan Head. He's done more for me than I could ever do for him.   I did do something once though."

"What did you do?"

"I saved his life."   He paused, reliving the moment.   "That was in the time of Suez.   We were just kids then really.   We were out on a raid one night, but they knew we were coming.   It was a mess.   We lost most of our unit on that one, but Tristan and I got out.   On the way back, one of their party must have got left behind.   Tristan was a little bit ahead of me. He came up behind Tristan but didn't see me. Thankfully, I saw him though – otherwise he would have got Tristan."

Anna turned over on the bed, listening.

"And we've been close ever since."

"Did you both stay in the army after that?"

"I got out five years later. Tristan had already left by then to start his building business. He looked after me and I did a few little jobs for him on the side."

A shadow crossed Anna's face that moment. There was the sound of a car outside slowly growling past and away.

"Did you hurt people, Noonan?"

"What?"

"I was married to a builder. I found out about the kind of people who would do 'a few little jobs' for him - some of them no better than low level thugs. I know the sort of things that go on. Did you ever kill anyone?"

Noonan looked at her, surprised. There was a blaze of anger in her eyes.

"No, Anna, I never killed anyone. That may have been your husband's way. It was never Tristan's."

"But you hurt people?"

"Only when they wanted to hurt Tristan. And very few of them ever tried to." She examined his face, searching for and finding the truth in it.

Anna lowered her body onto the bed and relaxed.

"What's your husband's name?" Noonan asked.

Anna hesitated.

"Come on, Anna. He's after both of us now, why keep it from me? What's his name?"

"Lee Mitchell. Have you heard that name before?"

"No, but Tristan certainly would have. He's in the same game after all. Look, if I can get to a telephone, I could speak to him. He might be able to help."

She looked at him for a moment, as if unsure where to begin.

"A year ago, I got enough evidence together against my husband to put him away for a long time. It was all there – bribery, corruption, murder. I kept it all together in a secret place. It's still there. Nobody else knows where it is, and I told no-one else what I was doing at the time. But still my husband somehow found out about it. Then he tried to kill me."

"If you really wanted to put your husband away, you could still do it with that evidence. If you told me where it is, we could go there together."

"I took it with me to Denby. It's still hidden away in my cottage."

Noonan let the air blow softly through his lips. Then suddenly his body was tense. There was the sound of a car hissing slowly past directly outside the building. Noonan motioned to Anna to stay on the bed. He leapt silently to his feet and crept to the curtain, peering carefully out onto the street. He could see the rear of a golden MGB moving stealthily along, its red rear lights glowing in the darkness. Then the car was gone and there was silence. Noonan turned back to Anna.

"That's the third time that car's driven past since we've been here."

Anna slowly sat up on the bed, understanding. Noonan and Anna remained poised in silence, staring at each other. The sound of voices could be heard from one of the neighbouring rooms, followed by a creaking floorboard. Then there was the sound of a car again. This time Anna herself was able to discern that this was the same car that she had heard a moment ago. Only this time, the car could be heard pulling up outside the hotel and stopping.

Noonan walked briskly to the light switch and snapped it out. He walked back to the curtains and looked through the crack. He saw the golden MGB parked right outside. The driver got out. Noonan recognised him immediately. He watched as the man looked the building over carefully. Then he walked to the front door. He tried the handle, but the door was locked.

The man stepped back out into the street and looked up at Noonan's window. Noonan stepped away from it and moved back towards Anna, who was now a black shadow in the dark room. The luminous hands of the clock on the bedside table told Noonan that it was 10.15pm.

Noonan sat down on the bed next to Anna.

"We need to get out of here," he told her quietly.

12

They waited until midnight, at which point Noonan was finally satisfied that the hotelier and his wife must be in bed. The MGB was still parked directly outside. It was impossible to see whether it was occupied. Noonan went to the door and opened it. He looked up and down the corridor which was shrouded in blackness. He could see and hear nothing. Anna was then at his side and the door clicked softly shut behind them. Noonan had to feel his way carefully along the wall to find his way. The floorboards groaned several times. Occasionally he brushed past the various alcoves along the way until he made it to the main staircase. Anna was holding on to his back. Noonan took Anna's hand and started to descend the staircase carefully. There was a dull glow of light at the bottom of the stairs which drew them to the reception area. The only way forward was into the rest room so Noonan guided Anna into it. The smell of tobacco still hung in the air.   There was another door heading towards the back of the building.   Noonan opened this and looked around.   This was evidently the kitchen.   The sound of a giant freezer unit hummed in the darkness and a small light shone out over the fridge.   Noonan felt around for a light switch.   Quickly his open palm brushed against something and the room was suddenly lit.

His luck was holding out.   The naked bulb hanging from the ceiling was giving out a dull light and there were no windows.   There was a wooden table in the centre of room and a door to the right. They walked in, closing the door behind them.

Anna watched as Noonan moved noiselessly to the refrigerator.   He opened it and started to remove various items. She had not been entirely comfortable with this part of the plan, as he had explained it to her earlier, but she could see that they had no choice.   Noonan would steal enough food to cover them for the next three days at least.   Additionally, he would look for a waterproof jacket for Anna.   He would need matches.   And whisky would be useful for keeping the cold out, though this was more for convenience.   Anna had made Noonan promise to leave adequate compensation for the items taken. Noonan had said that he would leave £2.50. Anna had forced him up to £5.00, which would have amounted to a considerable over-compensation. But Noonan had readily agreed; he had more important things to worry about.

Anna found a Sainsbury's plastic bag on the sideboard and filled it with the items that Noonan had taken from the fridge: ham and cheese sandwiches, fish, and cold meats. The sandwiches had clearly been prepared the previous evening, and had been wrapped in cellophane, perhaps for some of the other guests. Noonan had helped himself to them without hesitation. Anna grabbed some apples and bananas from a fruit bowl on the central table and dropped them into the bag also. Noonan carefully closed the fridge and moved to a set of drawers underneath the sink. He slowly opened each of them, leaving them open after examination. In the fourth drawer, he found the matches he was looking for. Simultaneously Anna was on the other side of the room opening cupboards. Leaning against the side of one was a whisky flask. She shook it, ascertaining that it was full.   Noonan and Anna dropped the matches and whisky into the bag on top of the other items.   Noonan nodded to her, indicating that he was satisfied.   She mouthed the word "money" at him. He shot her a slightly exasperated expression and pulled out his wallet, leaving the £5.00 on the central table by the fruit bowl.

A dull thud sounded from nearby. Anna froze and Noonan leapt silently to the light switch, shutting it off.   He grabbed Anna and pulled her to the door on the right, positioning them both behind it.   There came the steady shuffle of footsteps approaching. The sudden plunge into total darkness dazzled Anna.   There was the sound of the door clicking open and suddenly the room was lit again.   The heavy figure of the hotelier took a couple of steps into the kitchen.   He was wearing a crimson dressing gown and a pair of slippers.   He had what looked like a wooden truncheon in his right hand.   He looked suspiciously around.   Noonan silently cursed himself for not removing the Sainsbury's bag from the central table. It sat there like an enormous visiting card. The hotelier immediately spun around, raising his truncheon. Noonan quickly pushed the door shut and stepped forward.

"YOU...!" bellowed the hotelier. He brought the truncheon down hard. Noonan quickly ducked to the side, the truncheon slicing harmlessly through the air. He took a step back and then shot forward with the upper half of his body. He slammed his fist into the hotelier's face. The hotelier's body rocked momentarily before crashing heavily to the tiled floor. The truncheon clattered and rolled away to the side. The hotelier tried to lift his considerable bulk, moaned for a second, then dropped back to the floor and was still. Noonan quickly crouched down and checked his pulse. He turned to Anna and nodded.

Noonan grabbed the Sainsbury's bag and guided Anna through the door to the right. He flipped the lights off. The small hallway outside appeared to be the living quarters for the hotelier and his wife and was already lit. There was a row of hangers next to a narrow wooden staircase and a series of overcoats hanging in a row. A prominent yellow sou'wester was hanging up in front. Noonan grabbed this and handed it to Anna, who put it on.

A door to the right suddenly opened and the landlady emerged from a bedroom, also in a dressing gown. Her eyes widened into circles when she saw Noonan and Anna, and her mouth began to open. Before the scream could explode from her lungs, Noonan shot forward, clamping his hand over her mouth. Her pushed her hard against the wall.

"Sshhh!" he commanded her. He waited for a few moments. He reassured her with his eyes. After a few seconds, she nodded. Gently, Noonan guided her back into her bedroom and sat her down on the bed. She sat there, white-faced, looking back to him, unable to move.

"It's alright, I don't mean to harm you," whispered Noonan to her. "Your husband is in the kitchen. He's unconscious but he's going to be alright. Now there's a man out there who wants to kill us. Do you understand?" She nodded quickly. "We're on our way now. If you want to call the police after we've gone, that's up to you. There won't be any comebacks from us." She nodded one more time, the fear beginning to fade from her eyes. Noonan squeezed her shoulder once, then darted out of the room, grabbing a key from the door. He closed and locked it, leaving the key in the door. Anna was looking at Noonan uneasily.

"She's fine," he whispered.

Noonan quickly rolled up the Sainsbury's bag and shoved it into his rucksack. He put it on.

Opposite them was a metal door with a bar across it. Noonan opened it and a blast of cold air blew into the building. Noonan looked out into a courtyard. There was a washing line, two metal bins and not much else. There was a six-foot wall leading to a flat roof of a building about twelve feet high.

Noonan and Anna stepped outside, Noonan gently closing the door behind him. They moved noiselessly to the wall. Noonan cupped his hands and Anna placed her foot in them. She swung onto the wall and tiptoed along it. Noonan grasped the top of the wall with his hands and swung himself up. He followed Anna to the end. She reached up and lifted herself onto the roof. She looked back and Noonan was following her, twisting his body, and rolling himself onto the roof. They carefully got to their feet. Noonan put a hand to his mouth and motioned forward. They crept to the edge. Noonan dropped to his knees then lay forward on his

stomach.   Anna followed his movements.
Noonan peered over the roof and into the
street below.   There was a dark silhouette
waiting on the pavement with its back to
them.   One glance was all Noonan needed.
The long leather jacket and sideburns were
unmistakeable.   Noonan glanced at Anna
and she understood instantly.   They both
drew back silently, keeping two feet away
from the edge.   Noonan cupped his arms
into a diamond shape and stared into the
black void between them.   He cursed
silently. Every move that he made seemed
to be anticipated and countered by the
other man.   He was   unshakeable.
Noonan lifted his head and looked around.
There was nothing to the right.   Going
forward or backward was clearly out of the
question.   To the left was a sloping roof.
There was a three-foot gap separating
them and it was about two feet higher.
They would have to take it.   But how much
noise would they make landing on the roof?
And would the man hear?   Would he see?
The gradient of the roof was about forty-
five degrees.   Noonan nudged Anna with
his elbow and indicated over to it.   He slid
as quietly as he could to the edge, trying
not to dislodge any pebbles.   He could hear
a few of them rattle as Anna followed him.

He winced in irritation and closed his eyes. In the silence of the early morning the rolling of the pebbles sounded to Noonan as loud as pistol shots. He prayed that the man in the street below had not heard. It was just possible that he had not.

Noonan got to the edge and waited for Anna to catch up. He indicated across to the other roof. Noonan raised himself into a crouch and flung himself forward through the air. He landed elegantly on his feet in a crouching position and twisted around to face Anna. He waved his arm at her. She moved up into a crouching position and leapt forward too. Noonan grabbed at her as she landed on the roof. He thrust his arms around her waist and pulled her to him. They lay on their stomachs for several seconds in absolute silence. Noonan looked around. This section of the roof was mercifully still shrouded in shadow. Had the man heard? Noonan peered over his shoulder back towards the road. The black figure of the man stepped out into it and seemed to be looking all around. Noonan grabbed Anna's wrist and squeezed it. His navy-blue overcoat gave him good camouflage, but Anna's yellow sou'wester would be a dead giveaway. How much would the shadows cover them? The man stayed in this position for what seemed like agonising minutes. Noonan's mind screamed at the man to move. But still, he did not. The man turned and seemed to be facing them directly. Was he staring up at them? Had he seen them? The rucksack weighed heavily on Noonan's back as he lay there. Suddenly the figure moved forward and disappeared. Noonan pulled Anna up the roof and down the other side. There was a fifteen-foot drop into a garden. Noonan peered into the darkness trying to find a patch of visible grass. There was a square meter of it just to the right of them. Noonan judged the distance, crouched, and jumped into black, empty space. Three seconds later he landed with a thump in a patch covered in darkness. He bent his knees and rolled over onto the ground. He felt the cushion of soft, damp earth as he brushed against the ground. He had landed in a vegetable patch. He looked up for Anna, waiting with his arms in the air. She hesitated then jumped. She landed a couple of feet from his landing position. He picked her up.

"Are you OK?"

"I'm fine."

Noonan looked around. They were in a row of gardens separated by wire fences. The fence at the end was wooden. Noonan and Anna vaulted over the wire fences, crossing all the gardens until they got to the wooden fence. They heaved themselves over and dropped down the other side.

They were in the high street.

Noonan and Anna walked slowly and carefully through the shadows. The sea breeze was blowing in their faces. There was nothing else moving on the high street. They reached a corner and looked down a side street. There was a bright red telephone box, lit up and shining like a beacon in the darkness.

"Come on," he almost whispered to her. He grabbed her hand and they walked hurriedly but silently towards it. All the time he was looking up and down the street, but the empty darkness yawned back at him. They reached the telephone box. "I'll be as quick as I can," Noonan told her. "Keep out of sight!" He went inside the booth, shrugging off the rucksack and placing it at his feet. Anna pressed herself against the side of a building, keeping out of the light. She kept checking in both directions.

Inside the booth, Noonan felt horribly exposed. The light from the booth would have advertised his presence to anyone who happened to be passing at the end of the street. It also prevented him from being able to see anyone who might be approaching. He would just have to be as quick as he could. He began to dial the telephone number that was firmly stamped across his memory, the number that he could have recited in his sleep. He took out the last of his loose change. There were three 10p pieces, which was just enough for the call he needed to make. He let his finger fall away from the dial. He heard the blip of the telephone ringing in his ear. He turned to the side and stared at his ghostly reflection in the glass. The telephone continued to ring. Could Tristan be away on business, possibly abroad? Would Anastasia be with him if he were? But then there was a soft click, a moment's pause and then Tristan's voice – smooth, urbane, delicately precise, unmistakeable – speaking in his ear.

"Hello?"

The blips sounded in his ear. Noonan had had the coin ready in the slot and he pushed it in. Then he could hear Tristan's voice again.

"Hello?"

He could not keep the sleepiness out of his voice. The word almost came out like a yawn. Noonan waited a second and then spoke clearly and slowly into the mouthpiece.

"Tristan. It's Tom."

A pause.

"Tom?"

"I'm sorry for phoning at this hour. It's urgent. Can you talk?"

"Give me a moment."

The sound of dead air came through the receiver, gnawing away at him. His shrouded reflection stared back at him. He waited for what seemed like two minutes, which was interrupted only by the sudden blipping of the coin running out of time. Noonan clumsily pressed the second 10p coin into the slot. He had already used up a third of his phone money and the conversation had hardly got started. What the hell was Tristan doing? Making himself a cup of coffee? Noonan could picture the scene in Tristan's bedroom. Tristan turning on the reading light and slipping out of bed, Anastasia lying next to him half-asleep, her magnificent mane of thick blond hair splayed out all over her face, murmuring to

143

him, Tristan whispering to her to go back to sleep. Then finally Tristan came back on the line.

"Alright, Tom. Sorry about that. I'm in the study now. Didn't want to disturb Anastasia."

Tristan sounded wide awake now, his mind as alert as it always was. Noonan felt his heart warming at the sound of his old friend's voice. It was always a comfort to be talking to him.

"How are things, Tom?"

"A little hot right now. I've run into some trouble down in the west country."

"What sort of trouble?"

"I'm with a girl called Anna Raven. There's a man who's after us – and he's close."

"What the hell have you got yourself into, Tom?"

"Listen, Tristan. This girl Anna is married to someone you probably already know, and he sent this man after us. He's one of your competitors - Lee Mitchell."

"Oh, yes. I've had trouble with him before. He's up to his neck in it, believe me."

"Well, if you want to get Mitchell off your back, I've got something that might be useful. The girl put together some evidence to use against her husband and I know where it is."

"Great, can you get it?"

"Yes.   Once I've sorted out this other problem."

"Can I help?"

"Well, I'm running a little short of funds."

"Where are you exactly?"

"Some village along the northern coast of Devon.   A few miles upriver from Denby."

"Hang on."

The silence hung in the air for a few seconds.

"OK, I've got you.   How are you travelling?"

"Boat."

"OK.   Keep heading inland.   When you get to Ilfracombe, call me again.   I'll send some money to the Post Office there."

"Thanks, Tristan."

"No problem."

A pair of headlights turned into the road and shone brightly into the telephone booth.   Noonan instantly slammed the receiver back onto the cradle and pushed himself out through the door.   The car suddenly roared towards him and mounted the pavement.   Noonan was able to make out the sleek shape of the MGB. Anna came running out of the shadows.

"Noonan!" she screamed at him.

The MGB screeched to a halt. The door swung open and the man got out, leaving the engine running, the whites of his teeth flashing in the night like the fangs of a wild animal. His eyes were wide as saucers. He raced towards Noonan. In his hand was a hunting knife. Instinctively Noonan took off his overcoat and wrapped it up in his right arm. The man lunged towards him, the knife flashing out at him and cutting through the night air. Noonan jumped back, the knife missing him only by inches. Still the knife kept coming at him, scything through the air, and once connecting with his shoulder. Noonan felt the sharp slash of the knife as it ripped across his left shoulder followed by the warm rush of blood. Noonan inhaled sharply and retreated further down the street. The eyes and the teeth of the man took on an even greater look of wild intensity.

Behind the man, out of the corner of his eye, Noonan was able to see Anna leap into the MGB. Leaving the door open she rammed the MGB into first gear. The car shot forward. The man took a moment to

146

turn his head and his face was momentarily caught in the blaze of the headlights. His eyes and his skin shone whitely. A moment was all Noonan needed. He charged at the man, using every ounce of strength that his body could summon. His hands caught the man flat on the torso, pushing him out into the path of the oncoming car. His face momentarily registered the horror, the realisation of what was about to happen. Then he tried to jump out of the way. All too late. The bonnet of the car hit him square in the right thigh. His body briefly spun in the air. The man yelled out for a second like a wounded animal. Anna tried to reverse, crunched the gears, and stalled the car. The engine cut out and there was silence. The man rose into view, lit by the headlights, his eyes flashing with fury. Anna frantically felt for the ignition key and realised with horror that there was no key. She tumbled desperately out of the car and raced back down the street. Noonan grabbed the rucksack, put it on, and followed close behind.

The man, now shrieking in pain, hobbled to his car, and collapsed into it. He slammed the door. He fumbled in the blackness for the wires, hotwired it, and reversed the car back up the street after them at a terrifying speed. Noonan and Anna made it to the T-Junction. A van was coming up the main road at about thirty miles per hour. Noonan seemed to watch the spectacle in slow motion. The collision was grindingly inevitable. The boot of the MGB emerged out of the side road at the precise moment the van appeared. There was a sickening crunch of metal followed by the tinkle of broken glass dropping onto the tarmac. Noonan tore his eyes away. He took Anna's arm and pulled her along the main road towards the harbour. In the gloom he was able to pick out the wayfarer in the distance bobbing innocently and gracefully up and down. Behind him at the scene of the accident the sound of raised voices punched through the night air after them.

No-one but the van driver had been around at that time of the morning. And so, no-one ever saw the two exhausted figures climbing aboard the wayfarer and setting off across the dark, still waters into the blackness of night. Behind them the lights of the village twinkled at them like the eyes of an animal. The eyes seemed to be saying, *"We'll get you next time. Have no doubts about that."*

13

Tristan Head tiptoed back up the steep, narrow wooden staircase, holding onto the wooden bannister. It was an old manor house from the eighteenth century situated in the Surrey Hills in a tiny, beautiful little hamlet called Farley Green. A long drive with wooden picket fences on either side led up to the front door and the back of the house overlooked a magnificent, wide valley. He crept silently along the corridor, his mind suddenly churning with all too many questions for which there were no answers. He got to the bedroom door with an old-fashioned handle that is pressed with the thumb. He opened the door, hoping that Anastasia would be where he left her, asleep in the bed.

He was immediately disappointed but not surprised. Anastasia had an uncanny instinct for knowing when something was wrong. She was sitting on the edge of the bed with her white dressing gown around her and her long hair carefully brushed. She was looking up at him, beautiful, guarded, her sharp, emerald eyes burning with questions. Tristan stood in the door and closed it quietly. The bedside light was on. The room was all white and luxurious in its vastness and simplicity. A door on the other side of the room led to an en-suite bathroom, with a round, sunken bath. The bathroom was the same size as an average person's drawing room.

"What are you doing up?" Tristan asked, a hint of exasperation in his voice.

"You went all the way downstairs to take a call at half past twelve at night." She leaned forward. "It was Tom, wasn't it?"

"It's nothing for you to worry about," Tristan replied smoothly.

"Wasn't it?" she pressed.

"Yes, it was Tom," he admitted. He sat down on the bed next to her.

"Is he alright?"

Tristan turned and looked into his wife's eyes which were now sparkling with curiosity despite the uncivilised hour. He understood that evasion with Anastasia was futile. In all things, she already half-knew the truth and was just waiting for confirmation.

"He's in trouble. Somewhere in the west country…" Tristan went through every detail of the conversation as he recalled it, including the abrupt way the call was suddenly ended. Anastasia's eyes burned fiercely with intelligence as she absorbed everything that her husband had told her. She searched her husband's face for anything else that he might have been keeping from her.

Tristan Head was almost too beautiful to be male. He had thick, dark blond hair and a pair of soft, pale blue eyes that seemed to melt when they were being looked at. His voice however was crisp, refined, and commanded attention. He had spent a year at Sandhurst at the age of twenty before becoming an Officer in the army and seeing action overseas. His family had all had a history in the military, but Tristan had thrown away a whole promising career by turning away from the army and starting his own business. It had been the ultimate act of rebellion for which his family had virtually disowned him. In fact, he had rebelled his way since then towards a vast fortune and at the tender age of only thirty-seven had built for himself an enviable lifestyle that was equal parts hard work and hard adventuring. He had generated his large fortune dragging dusty, dreary cities into the future by developing and building exciting shopping precincts and apartment blocks.

Anastasia was his equal in most respects. With her luxurious mane of orange-blond hair, bright cat-like green eyes, statuesque frame, and hour-glass figure, she could have easily passed for one of those beautiful starlets that often turned up in low budget horror films. In fact, on more than one occasion, she had been likened to an apparently popular Australian actress working in the UK whose first name was Anouska. But Anastasia could never remember her surname. In fact, Anastasia had had a brief flirtation with the film world when she was in her early twenties. Her first job after leaving secretarial school had been at Pinewood Studios as a Production Secretary to a visiting American director. He had chosen her specifically from several candidates and she very quickly understood why as he never missed an opportunity to put his hand on her. On one occasion he even tried to seduce her with talk of getting her in front of the camera and building her up into a leading lady. She always managed to ward him off, but in time she started to find aspects of the film business rather desperate and degrading, so it was with some relief that she was finally able to leave the world of movies behind at the end of the film's production.

The next few years had seen several more top secretarial jobs, albeit in the rather more mundane world of big business. Her bosses in this new world had been straight-out-of-central-casting products of the public-school network. She gave everything to her work and for the most part enjoyed it, took pride in it, but was always aware that it would not lead her to where she felt she really needed to be. Her bosses always treated her with courtesy and respect. Some of them even still wore bowler hats and carried umbrellas on their way into the office.

During this time, Anastasia had begun two very brief love affairs, but she quickly realised that she had a zest for life and adventure that was not shared by her suitors. So, she had politely but firmly declined their proposals of marriage and sought refuge in her work. Anastasia had

Russian aristocracy in her blood and had very devout views about marriage. She had always believed that her one true love was out there, and she would wait for him. In the meantime, some of the younger executives, the types who tended to bomb around in sports cars at the weekends wearing cravats, often tried their luck with her. With them, she was often not quick enough to avoid the old problem of what she would describe as "wandering fingers with a vengeance". But she quickly became proficient in dealing with them. These kinds of young men were of no interest to her. Very quickly they would become trapped and bored by marriage and bitterly disappointed by respectability. She did not want a husband so much as a fellow adventurer in life. She found him in Tristan Head.

Her boss at the time, the rather grandly named Sir Miles Davidge, who looked and sounded as his name suggested, had tried to acquire – in a rather unorthodox manner – a property business run by a swaggering young upstart named Tristan Head, which had not been doing so well. A meeting had been arranged and she had been present as Sir Miles's secretary. Tristan had brought his own secretary. The moment Anastasia and Tristan set eyes on each other, they recognised that they were kindred spirits, fellow conspirators. It was a feeling that went much deeper than mutual attraction. They surreptitiously arranged a private meeting in a quiet hotel and restaurant on the river in Marlow, the Compleat Angler, and spent the rest of the evening – and then the rest of the night – thoroughly absorbed with each other. Treachery it may have been, but Anastasia went over to Tristan's side with no pangs of conscience. She worked her three-month notice period and during that time Sir Miles was always polite to her but suddenly distant. Suddenly she had become "Miss Charman" instead of "Anastasia". But the three months went by quickly enough and at the end of them she immediately became Tristan's new personal secretary, lover, partner and eventually his wife.

Tristan's wealth increased many times over the years. When he was not working, he was mountaineering, parachuting, rock climbing, pushing his body and mind to the limit to see what he was capable of. And Anastasia wanted to do it all with him. And she did. They were married within a year and were rarely apart from then on.

Then the first note of tragedy was struck in their marriage. After five years they decided the time was right to start a family. They tried hard for a child and Anastasia became pregnant twice but miscarried on both occasions. The second time she became withdrawn and depressed for long periods of time. She made a steady recovery but was never quite the same woman again.

Tristan and Anastasia became closely acquainted with some of the wealthiest and most glamorous couples in high society. But the one friend who mattered more to them than any was Tom Noonan. From Anastasia's point of view, he was the wild card in the pack. He was not wealthy and seemed to belong to a mysterious, shadowy world that was not open to her. She found him exciting. He reminded her of Tristan in so many ways and they seemed so tuned to each other that they might have been twins. Noonan however seemed to Anastasia a version of Tristan that had gone rogue. If Tristan had embraced the British establishment then Noonan very much stood apart from it. She never quite got to the bottom of what he did for a living. He would tell her that he was a Civil Servant and when she asked Tristan, he would say the same thing. She wondered if Tristan in fact knew more than she did but was keeping quiet about it. Certainly, Tom hardly ever talked about himself and she quickly learned not to ask too many questions. She surmised that he either did not want to talk about his work or was bound not to. She had her theories though. Given his love of the outdoors and his addiction to dangerous pursuits she found it increasingly hard to believe that he sat behind a desk for a living.

Tristan and Tom would try to meet once a month and Tristan would always keep a weekend free for his visits. There were some months when he was not able to make it as he was out of the country. That was something else that never quite tied in with the Civil Servant image. But Tristan clearly loved his weekends with Tom. And Anastasia came to love them too. The three of them together were a completely tight unit. They would take off in the Range Rover and go looking for thrills. One weekend they drove all the way up to the Scottish Highlands, having picked out a mountain that looked suitably dangerous and challenging. They spent another weekend deep sea diving off the Isle of Tresco. Often, they would spend their Saturday evenings huddled around a campfire in the middle of some woodland miles from anywhere. Anastasia strongly felt that Tristan was as close to Tom as he was to her. Over time, she also began to feel the same thing about Tom. She should have felt uncomfortable with this, but she did not. It felt entirely innocent and natural. If Tristan ever picked up on this it never seemed to bother him. Weekends with Tristan and Tom became the highlight of the month for her. Other weekends involved travelling up to town to attend charity balls and private functions with friends and wealthy clients. These she always enjoyed but never in the same way as the times she enjoyed with Tom.

Three incredibly happy years she had spent with Tristan and Tom. Then two things happened, and her life changed. She miscarried for a second time and Tom suddenly disappeared from their lives. If Tom had been there the first might have been easier to overcome. But he had not been. Suddenly the weekends stopped happening. He was suddenly not there. She always suspected that Tristan was still in contact with him, but she could never get him to admit to it. Tristan would not talk about it and became irritable if she pushed him. She had as much of a right to be in touch with Tom as he did. And now he had just been in touch again. Anastasia knew. She felt it. No-one else would have telephoned at that time of the morning. It could only have been Tom. And now Anastasia wanted to know as much as her husband. And Tristan on this occasion had known better than to try and keep the truth from her.

"We need to go down there," Anastasia told Tristan.

"No," Tristan replied.

"But he needs help!" she insisted.

"There's nothing we can do for him right now. I've said I'll send him some more money though."

"You know I think I met this Anna once. At Sotheby's. She was there with Mitchell. Four years ago, I think it was. Do you remember?"

"Sotheby's?"

"Yes."

"I can't remember her."

"Mitchell introduced me afterwards."

"What was she like?"

159

"Very young.   She reminded me of me – ten years back."

"Oh."

Tristan paused, lost in his own thoughts.

"Right, so what are we going to do about the Kidlington contract?" Anastasia prompted him.   She put her hand up to his hair, stroking it.   It was the first time she had done that for a while.   It made him smile and gave him a warm feeling.

"I'm going after Sir Lawrence Canning.   He's got in the way of my deals one time too many.   He sold me out to Mitchell.   I'm going to see him tomorrow. And if he's not where I'm expecting him to be,   I'll   find   him   somehow."

"Larry the Lizard?"

"Now, now," he admonished her with a sly grin.   He looked at his watch. "It's quarter past one.   And I don't think I'm going to be getting much more sleep tonight."

He smiled at her, pulled her towards him and kissed her gently on the forehead.

"Would you like coffee?" he asked her.

She smiled and nodded.

"Come on," he smiled, pulling her up from the bed. They walked to the door and went through. The door clicked shut behind them. The empty room seemed to ponder what had been discussed between them in deep silence.

14

A storm was moving quickly in a steady south-westerly direction. Tom Noonan could feel it coming. In the mid-afternoon gloom, the wayfarer ploughed on obstinately.

In the early hours of that morning, Noonan and Anna had used the outboard motor to get as far away from the town as they could in the pitch blackness. Five minutes out of the harbour they had come to a private beach not apparently accessible by road and had pulled the boat onto the sand. By the light of the lantern, Anna had had to tend to Noonan's bleeding shoulder. Noonan had talked her through the procedure. The slash of the knife had left a superficial shoulder wound. Nonetheless it had been bleeding profusely and could not be left. There had been a strong possibility of the wound going septic. If that had happened, Noonan would have required professional care which he was anxious to avoid. So, they

162

had had to take care of it themselves. Noonan blessed their good fortune in finding the whisky. At least it would guarantee a clean wound.

Anna had knelt in front of him and, following his directions, had poured whisky onto the wound. Noonan had grimaced in pain for a couple of seconds, but then the pain died down and it was over as quickly as it had begun. Anna had taken a handful of tissues from the rucksack and had pressed them firmly against Noonan's shoulder. Finally, they had lain down, side by side, on the tarpaulin and let sleep gradually overcome them. Noonan had draped his heavy overcoat over Anna to keep her as warm as possible and he had used the sou'wester as a pillow for her. He had neither a pillow nor coat over him, but he was used to that.

He had awoken with a start at 5.30am and had stared up at the stars, shivering in the cold air. His shoulder wound was throbbing slightly, but it was nothing serious. He had lost himself in the beauty of the stars and their formations and had thought of Anna. She had stirred an hour later and sat up. Their eyes had adjusted to the darkness and they had breakfasted on fruit and fresh meat.

Immediately Noonan felt strength returning to his body. After breakfast, Noonan had pushed the boat out onto the water, and they had set off on the next leg of their journey.

The blackness of the sky gave way to a murky grey and then light appeared on the horizon. Cloud formations gradually became visible in the dawn sky. By now they were both working the boat equally; no longer did Noonan have to instruct Anna through every step as she manned the jib, she seemed to be working it out on her own. Yesterday she had never sailed before, but now she was sailing as if she had been doing it for years. He felt a warm glow inside him.

And then, several hours later, Noonan suddenly felt a thick, fat drop of water land squarely on his forehead. He looked up at the sky, which was now suddenly covered with dark, oppressive thunder clouds.

"We're about to be hit by a storm," Noonan called out to Anna. Then the first heavy drops of rain landed on top of them. Anna nodded, covering her head with the hood of the sou'wester.

"We're going to get rocked about all over the place," Noonan called again. "So, hang on tight. And when you hear me call out "ready about!" you get your head down and you keep it down! OK?"

She nodded, a look of mild anxiety on her face. Noonan braced himself. It was not uncommon for bodies to tumble out of small dinghies in extreme weather conditions and be lost to the seas forever. Every year dozens of sailors who had bravely tested themselves against the ferocious might of the waters had been claimed by them, never to return. And Noonan understood that they were about to be thrown about in the waters like a bucket in a bathtub.

The rain then began to hammer down on them, and the clouds started to blacken. A thunderous crash rolled across the skies and a white flash lit up the horizon. Get ready, Noonan told himself. This is *it...*

They were frighteningly vulnerable in their tiny little dinghy on the rolling, choppy seas that stretched out all around them. The Bristol Channel has frequently been described as having some of the most treacherous and hazardous waters in the world. Well, now they were baring their fangs and growling out their disdain to them.

The boat was being mercilessly rocked about as the turbulent waters rose and fell around them like a living, breathing monster. A huge wave soared upwards in front of them. The dinghy hit it and was thrown up into the air at a forty-five-degree angle. Water showered into Noonan's face and he squinted to maintain clarity of vision. He felt the salty taste of water in his mouth. Anna let out a cry and heaved on the jib. Both sails were taking the full force of the incredible winds.

"Hang on!" Noonan shouted out needlessly. Anna gave no indication of having heard him in the cacophonous roar of thunder and rain. But she was hanging on alright. Hanging on for dear life. They reached the crest of the wave and suddenly Noonan felt the sickening plunge in his stomach as the dinghy plummeted downwards. Then they were being hit from the port side and the main sail was suddenly swinging across towards Anna.

"READY ABOUT— LEE-HO!" roared Noonan as loud as he could. Anna turned to him as if not quite understanding. Then she sensed the main sail soaring towards her at a terrifying speed. In the nick of time, she ducked, and the main sail locked into position inches above her head. The boat was forced to change direction and jibe by the winds now blowing them hard from port side. The wind was so fierce that it lifted the side of the boat upwards as it cut through the waters. Noonan was thrown sideways and felt his head hitting the water. For a second, he had gone under, the world suddenly turning black, all noise cut out. A hand grabbed his wrist and pulled him back up. Noonan looked up and saw Anna leaning forward, her left arm still pulling on the jib, her right arm pulling him. He got to his feet.

"Reef the sails in!" he roared. She looked back at him, shaking her head, not quite understanding. "Pull them in!" he called out again. She then pulled desperately at the jib and he grabbed at the main sail. Very quickly the boat levelled out. Noonan looked over to starboard and saw the blackness of the mainland jutting out of the water. They were about half a mile offshore. A terrible thought suddenly seized Noonan. The rucksack! He looked desperately around and instantly breathed a sigh of relief. Anna had had the foresight to shove the rucksack tightly into a corner of the dinghy and mercifully it was still there. They would have to make sure they did not lose it.

There was only one course of action available to them. They would have to make it to shore as quickly and as safely as possible. The bad news was that being in a wayfarer they were entirely at the mercy of the winds. The good news however was that the winds were blowing them towards the shore. If they could maintain a straight line, they should reach it in about ten minutes.

Noonan and Anna gently let the sails out a little and the boat obliged them by moving in a roughly straight line. But the boat was being buffeted fiercely around and was rocking back and forth. The sail was swinging precariously, and Noonan was heaving at it to keep it under control. The rucksack began to roll around in a semicircle at the front of the boat. Noonan never took his eyes off it and his body remained poised, ready to dive for it as it edged closer to the side. The wind blew into Noonan's ears with explosive force. Sheets of rain were now smacking into his eyes. But their luck held out and the dinghy rocked up to the shore.

Suddenly, there was a loud crash, and the boat was starting to fill with water.

Almost immediately it was now up to Noonan's ankles. Anna was slipping around in the water as the boat blew from side to side. A rock had torn an ugly great gash in the side of the boat. They were running out of time.

Noonan leapt out of the boat, splashing into the freezing, foaming waters, and pulled it towards the shore. Anna quickly jumped over the other side and pulled from her end. They waded through the water which swirled around them like black treacle. Soon it was only up to their heels and then they were crashing through damp sand, dragging the boat with them. They made it to the middle of the beach and let it go, the boat hovering uncertainly for a moment before toppling clumsily onto its left side. Noonan stepped back and examined the damage; a ferocious hole had been torn in the side of the boat, and it was now useless. Working at a furious pace, he took the main sail and the jib down, laying the outboard motor on top of them. He grabbed the rucksack, jumped out and stepped away. The dinghy lay forlornly on its side, like a panting animal in need of a rest. Noonan put the rucksack on his shoulders, took Anna's hand, and they ran up the beach towards a chalky path leading up a hill.

A milky river was rushing down the track from the top of the hill. Noonan and Anna slipped and struggled up the path, eventually making it to the top. They were looking out across a valley. Hills rose further inland and a single muddy track wide enough for a car stretched on into the distance. A wooden barn stood near the top of the hill on a stretch of level ground several yards away to the right. They ran to the barn as the rain lashed furiously at them.

They tumbled through the entrance and looked around. Bales of straw stretched up to the ceiling. The rain drummed ominously on the roof. They made their way towards the back of the barn and then collapsed onto a bale of straw laid horizontally on the ground. Noonan peeled his now sodden naval overcoat off and Anna tore at her sou'wester, letting it fall in a dripping heap. Then Anna was clawing at Noonan's sweater and shirt and ripping them off. He found that he was doing the same thing with her grey sweater. Noonan was too exhausted and numb from the cold for his brain to really process what they were doing. Their bodies had taken over and were acting in accord with their untethered emotions.

Freezing, shivering, beaten to the core, Noonan and Anna wrapped their legs around each other and hugged each other tightly. They were welded together now, one unit. The skins of their chests clung wetly together. The warmth from their bodies flowed into each other, giving them strength. She laid her head on his shoulder and he pressed his nose into her thick curtain of hair. Their bodies shook together in coldness and relief. They never knew how long they stayed like that. For Noonan had quickly closed his eyes and let the shackles of time slowly slip away from him.

The darkness had crept in on them virtually unnoticed. When Noonan finally opened his eyes hours later, he was virtually blind. There was no light coming from anywhere. He could feel Anna's body still pressed into his. Her breathing had become even and steady. She had fallen asleep. Noonan gently laid her down on the straw and carefully unravelled himself from her. He felt around for the rucksack, found the matches inside, and pulled them out. He struck a match which flared up, lighting the barn in a flickering orange glow. He needed to get a fire started.

Any wood that was outside would be wet and therefore no good to him. His only hope was the possibility that there was dry wood inside the barn. He went through five matches before he found the chopped logs piled up at the other end of the barn. He collected ten of these along with some straw and took them outside. He looked at his watch. It was nearly midnight.

The rain had eased off, but he could still feel the odd drop. The musty smell of sodden earth hit his nostrils and he breathed it in for a moment, enjoying it. He arranged the logs and straw in a pile and lit another match. The straw caught and Noonan drew the logs into the flames. Immediately they started to leap up and smoke started to rise. He waved his hands, fanning the flames. Within five minutes the fire was popping and crackling, the intense heat warming Noonan's face and body.

He felt a movement behind him and looked up. Anna sat down, putting her arm around his shoulders, and leaning into him. He put his arm around her waist and smiled at her.

"Thank you," he said to her.

"For what?" she asked, surprised.

"The boat," he replied. She simply smiled, leaned in, and kissed him softly, once, on the lips. Noonan lifted his hand and ran it through her hair. His stomach suddenly growled at him.

"Food," he said to her softly and ran back for the rucksack. A little water had seeped into the sandwiches, making them a little soggy, but there were quite edible. The apples of course were fine. There were also thick slices of beef, which Noonan and Anna warmed over the fire with sticks. It was hardly a grand meal, but the beef from the fire came out piping hot, and all of it washed down with a welcome shot of warm, soothing whisky. The fire had by now dried his clothes completely and Noonan was feeling strong again. He handed the flask to Anna.

"Is this stuff any good?"

"Try it."

She put the flask to hcr lips and took a long gulp. She should have choked on it, but she simply let out a satisfied gasp.

"Don't develop too much of a taste for it, will you?"

She offered the flask back to him like a repentant schoolgirl. He took it, screwing on the lid tightly.

An hour and a half later, the fire was burning itself out and a long trail of smoke was stretching into the sky.

Noonan was asleep on a pile of corn. Anna lay a few feet away from him. Beyond the smouldering red logs outside the barn there was only blackness. And once again, in his dreams, the demons had come for Noonan. The body on the beach, crawling, bleeding. The face blackened, unrecognisable. The four men who stood over him, beating him, watching him dying. The man on the beach raised his head. His eyes were screwed shut. He opened his mouth and tried to scream...

On the straw, Noonan suddenly yelled out and opened his eyes.

Anna was kneeling over him. She was watching him tenderly, concern in her eyes.

"Noonan?"

Noonan exhaled slowly, remembering where he was.

"You were crying out. What is it?"

He shook his head. "Just a dream. Nothing to worry about."

She smiled. Then she lowered herself onto him, gently stroking his head. She leaned into his ear and whispered.

"Don't talk anymore."

And then she gave herself to him fully, kissing him firmly on the mouth. He wrapped his arms around her and squeezed her to him. And he gave himself to her fully in return. All the way through the night.

15

The bathroom felt as cold as a mortuary. There was a tiny window above a lavatory that was sealed shut. Despite that it was still freezing in there.

It was two o'clock in the morning. The storm had raged all evening and Jarrett had lain on the bed staring up at the ceiling, his left arm cushioning his head. His right thigh throbbed like a metronome with pain. If he twisted his body or moved a fraction, a vicious stab of pain would flash through his body.

The rain had drummed furiously and mercilessly on the roof of the small hotel that he had checked into earlier that evening. It was an old building and the roof had obviously not been maintained. He watched numbly as a patch of water gathered through a crack on the ceiling. Then the drips started, landing a few inches from the end of the bed. His mind was occupied with only one thing – finding the man and the woman who had escaped from him. He would kill the man and force her to watch it. Then he would take her back to Mitchell.

Drip, drip, drip...

Hours seemed to crawl by. And the soft, steady torture of the drips built up in his mind. His fists clenched and his jaw tightened. His body started to writhe on the bed.

Thud, thud, thud...

Time to get up!

Jarrett sprang off the bed and stood bolt upright in the room. He immediately felt better again. His mind was clear, his purpose once again driving him forward. A leak in the ceiling had resulted in a large, watery stain on the red carpet that was spreading. But Jarrett felt no need to look for a bucket or report the fault. If he had been an ordinary traveller or a tourist, he would have had good cause to complain. But he was no ordinary traveller.

He had looked at his watch then and seen that it was two o'clock in the morning. He had been on the bed for six hours, trapped and tormented by his thoughts. He had limped to the bathroom and turned the light on. He slowly, methodically, removed all his clothes until he was down to his underpants. He lifted his right leg onto the rim of the bath, pulled down his trousers and looked at his thigh. It was a gruesome, bloody mess. The surface of his skin had suffered numerous abrasions and blood had soaked through. An ugly purple sphere had grown around the bloody patches and beyond that, an ugly black bruise was spreading down his leg.

From an overnight case he extracted a small bottle of whisky and a roll of thick adhesive tape. He unscrewed the lid of the bottle and carefully poured whiskey all over his wounds. His right thigh was suddenly on fire. His mouth stretched wide open and he let out a silent, breathy roar. And then steadily the pain subsided. He picked up the adhesive tape and began to twist it round his leg, covering up the wounds, pulling tight. Satisfied, he tore the end off and chucked the tape down.

He hobbled to a mirror covering a small cabinet and stared at his own reflection for a few seconds. His eyes had become bloodshot after two sleepless nights. As the black, empty wells stared back at him, he reflected on the events of the past twelve hours.

The driver of the truck who had collided with him had got in his way and paid for it with his life. He had had the impression of a large, lumbering, slow-witted local man with thick curly hair in denim dungarees and an anorak. He had immediately laid into Jarrett with a furious torrent of verbal abuse, all delivered in a thick, west country accent. Jarrett had silenced him with one swift, vicious punch to the chin. The man had dropped to the ground. The anger had been throbbing remorselessly up through Jarrett's veins then and he had walked up to the truck driver, grabbed his head, and effortlessly snapped his neck with one smooth jerk. He had felt the life draining out of the man's body and simultaneously the anger had gradually subsided. He had immediately felt better. He had let the dead body drop to the ground and had left it under the truck with the engine still running.

He had driven through the black night, taking roads that ran as close to the coast as possible. He pressed on grimly through the wild, harsh, unforgiving countryside, stopping at every local town close to the coast but there had been no sign of the man and the girl. Then by the late afternoon the storm had set in and his stomach was screaming at him for food. His head was starting to throb with the ache that comes from lack of sleep. By six o'clock the storm had intensified to such a degree that it would have been impossible for his quarry to have continued by boat. So, when he had come across the small hamlet nestled snugly at the bottom of the valley he had decided to stop and rest.

He had quickly found the small hotel opposite the tavern, where he had called in for a meal of scampi and chips. The hotel was in such a dilapidated state that it was ashamed to even advertise its presence, right down to the measly one star on its board. So, he had checked into this pitiful hotel where he had spent the last few hours. The pasty faced, overweight proprietress had taken a whole minute to come out and meet him when he had sounded the bell. There was no warmth or welcome when she had appeared. She had obviously been startled by his appearance and had glanced curiously at him as he had struggled up the stairs. He had mumbled something about being accidentally knocked off his bicycle by a car, which she had ignored. The old bitch. He had watched the back of her fat, hairy neck as he had followed her along the dusty corridor. He had imagined snapping it like a twig. It would have been so easy. It would certainly have been a pleasure, possibly even an act of mercy. The thought cheered him slightly. Then she had shown him the room and left as quickly as she could.

He had gone straight to the bed and lain down. He had had the impression that there were no other guests. Nobody in their right mind would even consider staying in such a filthy place. There was presumably a large, rumbustious family living downstairs consisting of several adult sons. All evening he could hear them rowing with each other, while the image of the man he had sworn to kill grew sickeningly in his imagination.

At seven o'clock precisely Jarrett opened his eyes, having slept for five hours. He packed his things and left the room, never once glancing back. He took the stairs carefully. She was waiting for him at the bottom, her eyes filled with hostility and suspicion.

"I'll be on my way now," he told her, avoiding her gaze.

"Five pounds and fifty pence," she told him flatly. He paid her quickly and turned away. He walked to the front door and left the miserable place. His car was parked further down the street opposite a village store. He examined the state of it in the cold, grey light of the morning. The rear right end had been badly smashed in the collision and the metal had been bent inwards. The indicator lights had been smashed out and were useless.

The car was close to a wreck, but it would have to do. The driver's window was missing, and the rain had left the inside of the car soaking wet. It was of little consequence to Jarrett. He got inside, hotwired the car again and set off.

Ten minutes further down the road, he pulled into a small layby. He got out carrying a crowbar. He levered away with it until he heard the squealing sound of the lock being torn away. The lid of the boot sprang up. He leaned in and lifted a blanket concealing a long, brown leather case which contained a Remington Model 700 snipers' rifle complete with telescopic sight. He released the catch and peered inside. The early morning light of the day was briefly reflected off the highly polished stock and black barrel. He snapped the lid shut again. Alongside it lay a duffle bag. He reached inside and felt for the Sig P210 automatic pistol.   He weighed it in his hand before dropping it back in the bag. He threw both items into the backseat and sat back in the driver's seat.   He reasoned that the man and the girl could not have covered more than forty miles by boat the previous day, so he had to be close.   He slammed the door and pulled away, the car roaring down the road in a blast of smoke.

Five miles away to the north-west, Noonan was drowsing happily in the comfortable state that existed between sleep and full consciousness.   The memory of the girl's body on his massaged his mind. She had made love with the same fearlessness and wild abandonment with which she had faced the dangers of the last two days.   There had been no politeness, no tentative restraint in the way she had given her body to him.   He had felt her warm, soft body pressing down on his, her thick thatch of hair rhythmically brushing against the side of his face and her lips as she tenderly explored every part of his body.   And once she had exhausted everything, he had turned her over and given it all back to her until sleep had finally caught up with them.

He opened his eyes finally.   He could no longer feel the girl on top of him and could not see her anywhere. The cold light was shining through the entrance of the barn. Very quickly he lifted himself up and hurried outside. There she was, standing a few feet away, her back to him, just looking out across the valley. She did not turn to look at him. He came up alongside her. She reached out to him and clasped his hand and they stood there together for a moment.

When he finally spoke, his voice sounded oddly distant.

"I think it's time we told each other everything. Don't you?"

She turned to him slowly and smiled.

"I grew up by the water," she began. "That's why I ended up back there. That's home for me."

Noonan sat down on a bank and waited.

"I grew up in Margate. My childhood wasn't really a happy one. My father was a travelling salesman who was hardly ever there, and my mother had a part time job working in a tobacconist. There was never much money, so we never had very much." She shrugged. "When I was old enough, I decided to go to college. I had a weekend job which paid my way.

After that I went on to secretarial school. I learned shorthand, typing skills, the whole thing. I became confident and for the first time in my life I felt I really had a purpose. I applied for a job in London and got it. As soon as I could afford my first flat, I moved out of Margate and settled in London. Well, I hung around with all the other girls in the office. I learned from them how to dress, how to cook, where to go to meet all the *nice boys.*" She suppressed a small laugh. "So, life was good for a while. I was out on my own and making a good life for myself.

"Then it happened. I fell in love. With a man named Lee Mitchell. I got a job with his company in the secretarial pool. And that's how it all started. He happened to notice me and asked me out. It's funny. He was wonderful in the early days. He was much older than me, of course, a man with his own construction company. He seemed to have it all. He was handsome, he made me laugh - he had a wicked sense of humour. We went on some wonderful holidays together. And we fell in love.

"Not long after that, he asked me to marry him. He didn't need to ask me twice. So, we married. It was after the honeymoon that it all started going wrong. He would come home and be moody, worried, withdrawn. I couldn't get through to him. When I tried, he would just become angry, hostile – and I drove him further away. It was hard, but I kept going.

"Then one day while I was out shopping, I was accosted by a strange man. He identified himself as a police officer. We went to a quiet spot and we talked. A business associate of Lee's had gone missing. Did I know anything? He turned up dead later. I asked Lee but he was all innocence. Then the police officer turned up again on another occasion when I was out with a lady friend. Two more associates of Lee were also missing. Surely, I must know something, or have seen something? But I could not help. Sure enough, the bodies of those two men turned up later, in a car at the bottom of a quarry. The next visit I had was from a more senior man. He showed me his card and told me that Lee had been under suspicion for some time of fraudulent practices, intimidation and now he had possibly ordered the killings of these three men. He gave me a special telephone number, asked me to keep an eye out for anything suspicious and to ring the number if I had any information.

"I then became very, very frightened. Lee and I stopped talking to each other. I tried to stay as far away from him as I could. But I also was curious. I needed to know. So, I began to follow Lee. I built up a sort of dossier on him, recording all the places he went to, the people he would meet. I was going to present it to the senior policeman as soon as I had everything I needed. I had his number after all. When Lee was on the telephone at home, I would listen in on the other line, making notes. I was terrified all the time, but I was also elated, exhilarated. It was strange. And after a while I had enough in my dossier to present to the police. It may have been enough to get him arrested, who knows?

"So, I telephoned the number and agreed to meet the senior policeman. Just to be careful though, I hid the dossier in a place where I knew it could never be found. Then, the night before my meeting, Lee confronted me at home. He had somehow found out what I had been doing. Well, he knocked me about a bit. And then he said he was going to kill me, seeing as I had betrayed him. I'd never seen him like that before. It was as though he had gone completely mad. I was terrified but I managed to escape. I got in my car and I drove and drove, all through the night. And I didn't stop until I reached Denby.

"So, I started my life again. No people. No excitement. Just a job in the local shop and a quiet life. It worked. For a little while anyway."

"Until he found you."

She nodded. "Yes. And that was also the day that you found me. And that's my story."

"The man who's after us. Did you ever see him before?"

"Only the one time. And that was the night before Lee found out about me. Lee met him in a deserted car park, somewhere in Brentford, I think." She paused and shrugged. "Now it's your turn."

Noonan knew that he had to tell her something. But it was dangerous for him to tell her anything. Yet she had openly told him her story and he owed her at least some of the truth. But how to tell her? And how much?

He heard himself saying to her, "Tom Noonan died a year ago."

16

The small hamlet nestled cosily in a green valley surrounded by three hills. A long track led into the hamlet, which joined a B road a quarter of a mile away. The storm from the previous day had given way to a chilly, graceful day with blue skies and bright sun. There were only six buildings in the tiny hamlet, two barns, and four two-storey dwellings which housed four families.

The sound of west country folk music drifted up into the hills from the hamlet. The storm had made a quagmire of much of the surrounding countryside, but the courtyard in the centre of the hamlet had gravel on the ground and had remained dry. A small duck pond stood unobtrusively away to the left. A folk band made up of ten musicians played a jaunty, traditional folk tune called "The Durham Rangers". There were three accordion players, two grey-haired men and a smiley, middle-aged lady in a thick pair of spectacles. Two wholesome girls, with fresh, innocent faces and beatific smiles, not long out of their teens, scraped away at their violins. A slightly older woman, with a third violin, leaned forward and played, a look of fierce concentration on her face. The rest of the band was made of a clarinet, a banjo, a guitar, and a bongo drum. There were twenty-two people in the gravel courtyard. Some were dancing, others helping with the preparation of a huge feast on tables that were lined up along the side.

Everyone was too preoccupied to notice two distant figures appear from the peak of the highest hill and begin climbing down a path towards the hamlet. Noonan and Anna had been walking for five long hours and had covered ten miles. It had been ten o'clock when they had started out, following a full breakfast of meat, fish, and fruit, and it was now approaching three o'clock. Anna's thighs were throbbing with the ache of a long ten-mile walk. Her face was flush with warmth, and she could feel small droplets of sweat starting to run down her back. There had been several hills to climb and she was badly out of practice. The last two miles had been hard, and she was sorely looking forward to a rest and something to eat. Despite this however, she had felt happy. The wild, rolling countryside seemed to hold a romantic promise for her that filled her with excitement. Added to that was the thrill of being with Noonan. Standing atop the high hills with the wind blowing around her hair, she felt as though they could have been the last two people alive on Earth.

His revelation to her had been turning over and over in her mind as she had walked: "Tom Noonan died a year ago." She had pressed him as far as she had dared, but he had eventually lapsed into silence, and she could get no more out of him. Curtly, he had suggested that they begin their walk. The walking clearly relaxed him though, and he was in far better spirits only minutes later. But the peculiar revelation only made her feel closer to him than before, and she was determined to get to the bottom of his story, and, if possible, give him all the comfort and support that she could.

And what of the man who was still out there after them? How far behind was he now? Could he possibly find them out here? Perhaps they had lost him after all? She had *hoped* with all her heart that they had lost him, then she had promptly pushed the matter to the back of her mind.

Noonan, for his part, had also found temporary peace and solace in the hills. He had imagined himself and Anna as two lovers out for a Sunday stroll. Maybe they had been to church in the morning, followed by a Sunday roast, and were now walking it off. Then, back for tea and muffins at five o'clock, and possibly a thriller on television. These pictures played out in Noonan's mind. When all this ghastliness was over, this was all he would ever wish for. He would even go to church with her on Sundays. What a quaint idea! Noonan had never attended a church service. He had never in fact had any thoughts or beliefs in that direction whatsoever. But he could certainly see himself going to church with Anna. God! He must be changing!

The gradient down toward the hamlet was steep and Noonan held Anna's hand as they carefully descended. The cheery sound of the folk music floated up towards them. There was a stile at the bottom of the hill, and they climbed over it. With their leg muscles fiercely aching, they staggered wearily towards the centre of activities. They stood to the side and watched, as the locals milled about with food, while others danced, and the band played on.   Anna looked at Noonan, a smile of relief and curiosity playing across her face.   He shrugged in reply.

An attractive girl in her mid-twenties with long, straight black hair and a far-away look in her eyes, was making straight for them, darting in and out of the dancers.   She was looking straight at Noonan as she approached.

"Where have you come from?" she asked, her west country accent so thick that Noonan struggled to understand her.

"Fifteen miles downriver," Noonan replied in a non-committal manner.

"Where are you going?"

"How far's the next town?"

The girl pointed vaguely into the distance. "A few miles that way." The girl continued to look at Noonan with a far-away stare.   Then a smile slowly spread across her face.   "Would you like something to eat?"

Anna answered for them.   "Thank you, we're starving."

The girl beckoned to them, stifling a giggle.

"Please – come and eat."

She led them over to the tables where the food was being laid out. The women behind the tables fixed them both with sickly-sweet smiles that seemed to Noonan a little too forced. The plump lady closest to Noonan, her hair tied back in a tight bun, carelessly shovelled some chicken and bread onto a plate and handed it to him.

"You've just arrived?"

"Yes."

"You must be very hungry."

"Yes, thank you."

Noonan took the plate. One of the lady's similarly smiling companions handed Anna a plate. Anna thanked her and they turned away, watching the dancing. Anna looked at Noonan and noticed that his face was fixed in concentration. They ate in silence for a few moments.

"Noonan, what's the matter?"

"I don't know," he shrugged. "Maybe nothing."

"Well, I'm glad for the chance to rest and have something to eat," she replied. "I wonder what the occasion is?"

Noonan looked at her and shook his head.

"Oh, come on, Noonan, relax. These seem like good people." She continued to eat hungrily. At that moment, the girl with the far-away look appeared in front of Noonan, smiling coyly.

"Dance with me?" she invited him.

"No, I..." Noonan began.

"Dance with me," repeated the girl, her eyes flashing mischievously. Without waiting for a reply, the girl suddenly took Noonan's plate, placed it on the ground, grabbed his wrist and pulled him forward into the throng of dancers. The girl put her arm around Noonan's back and took his hand. Noonan reluctantly started to move with the girl in time to the music. He looked into her eyes, which were blazing with life and laughter. Then he turned and looked at the other dancing couples all around him, unable to shake an uneasy feeling that continued to gnaw away at him.

Anna watched Noonan dancing with the girl and laughed quietly to herself as she ate. A little girl, aged about eight years old, appeared at her side, reached up and tugged at her sou'wester. She looked down into the smiling face of the little girl. A moment later, three more children appeared. She knelt and talked to them.

Noonan, lost in the throng of the dancers, glanced over to her. Their eyes met briefly, and she shrugged happily at him.

The music, with its repetitive refrain, seemed to be swirling round and round Noonan. He began to feel slightly dizzy. But then the song ended with a rousing climax, followed by a round of applause. Noonan looked over to Anna, who was now sitting cross-legged with the children and playing a game with them. Noonan looked out to the track leading away from the hamlet, which disappeared round a bend after one hundred yards. Three trucks were parked near it. More than ever now, he was feeling the need to get moving. The possibility of the man finding them here was only part of what was bothering him. The rest he could not explain.

The band started playing again. The girl made a grab at Noonan's shoulders, but Noonan removed them and shook his head.

"No more," he told her firmly, and gently pushed her away. Her eyes briefly blazed at him and then went dull. He turned and made his way through the throng of dancers towards the trucks. He nonchalantly sidled up to them and, as casually as possible, peered through the driver's windows of all three. There were no keys inside any of them, and consequently no quick and easy way out of the hamlet by truck. Noonan looked back towards the music to make sure he was not being watched. The merriment and the dancing carried on innocently. Noonan then strolled casually towards the buildings and disappeared around the side of them. Anna immediately stood up and followed him, leaving the children to their game.

At that moment, a golden MGB appeared round the corner and growled to a halt next to the three trucks. Jarrett's distant figure climbed out of the car. He was limping heavily. He approached the congregation and watched them blankly for a few moments. Then he limped over to a small group and started asking them questions. One of the men listening to him nodded slowly.

Noonan walked carefully along the side of the building. He looked in through the window of one of the houses. An elderly lady sat in an armchair sewing. The windows were filthy with dirt and did not look as though they had been cleaned for years. Cobwebs criss-crossed across the room. Had it not been for the act of sewing, the elderly lady might have appeared to be dead.

Just then Noonan felt a tap on his shoulder. He turned in surprise and found himself staring at the young girl. Her eyes were now hard and challenging.

"I saw you by the trucks," she told him in her thick west country accent. "You were going to steal from us?"

"No," Noonan told her.

"I'll tell them," she threatened. But then she unbuttoned the top of her blouse and pushed herself up to him. "I'll tell them," she said again, more softly.

"No," Noonan told her again, more forcefully. The girl shrieked and slapped him. Noonan blinked once. The girl moved to slap Noonan a second time, but suddenly Anna was in between them, and grappling with the girl. The girl started to kick and scratch at Anna's face. Anna raised her hand and quickly slapped her across the face. A flash of fury burned briefly in the girl's eyes, followed by tears. The girl put her hand up to her cheek, then suddenly turned and ran back towards the congregation.

"Come on," Noonan urged Anna. "I think we've worn out our welcome here!"

They turned and started to walk quickly away from the sound of the music. They turned the corner of the building.

And froze.

Stepping out in front of them with an impassive look on his face was the man.

The Sig P210 was in his hand.

The sound of the folk band from the other side of the building suddenly cut out.

All was silent for a moment and nothing moved.

Noonan grabbed Anna and pulled her back. They raced to the nearest door and Noonan pulled it open. Mercifully, it was not locked. They rushed through the corridor of a house, Noonan slamming doors behind him as he ran. They made it to the front door and Noonan threw it open. They rushed out.

The congregation was spread out in front of them, but their kind and welcoming expressions from earlier had been replaced with outright hostility. As Noonan and Anna ran through them, they crowded in on them, punching, and shrieking obscenities in their faces. Noonan felt a glob of saliva smack into his face. He squeezed Anna's wrist, pulling her through the pile of bodies. For a few moments they were lost in a riot of fists, kicks, and screams.

Then they were free and away from them. Two shots exploded behind them and suddenly the crowd were screaming and running for cover. Noonan glanced quickly back and saw the man racing across the courtyard after them, his gun raised. Noonan and Anna threw themselves into a barn building on the other side as two more shots smacked into the wood close to Noonan's head.

They made it to the other end of the barn just as the man was entering. There was a hole at the back of the building. Noonan pushed Anna through and dived after her.

Noonan looked around. Stretching up a steep hill ahead of them was a dirt track. He pulled Anna forward. They scrambled over an iron gate and started to run up the steep track. Noonan felt a bullet crash into the top rung of the gate and ricochet away with a mournful whine.

Noonan looked back and immediately felt a wave of nausea. The man was limping terribly, and obviously in considerable pain, but somehow this did not slow him down. He was also armed and obviously a crack shot. The last shots had missed him only by inches.   Fear started to gnaw away at his gut.

Beside him, Anna was gasping in pain.   Every muscle in her legs felt smashed to pieces following the ten miles they had covered earlier in the day.   But the terror and the adrenalin pushed her firmly forward.

Noonan looked up to the top of the track and could see what looked like a farm building just beyond a hedge at the top. Behind them, the man carelessly squeezed off two more shots while he limped along, but the shots went wide of their targets.

Noonan pulled Anna harder up the slope.   He was suddenly aware of how exhausted his body felt.   He felt his heart exploding in his chest.   But the farmhouse gave him hope.   And hope gave him the final reserve of desperate energy to get him there.   Anna felt it too.   Facing down all the pain that was right now soaring through their bodies, they ran as hard as they had ever run in their lives to the top of the hill.

From there they could see the track leading down to a road.   There was a drive on the right leading into a farmhouse. They could hear a large vehicle of some kind being started up somewhere on the farm. It was the most beautiful sound that Noonan had ever heard. They started to run downhill. Just as they reached the drive, the vehicle appeared. It was a large cattle truck of some kind. It turned to the right and started driving down the hill.

"NO!" screamed Noonan. *"WAIT!"*

But the cattle truck kept going. Noonan and Anna raced after it, five feet behind it, now no longer aware of the pain they were in. But the truck just kept getting further away from them...

Jarrett made it to the top of the hill. His leg felt like his thigh had a hundred knives stuck in it, but pure determination had made him run faster than he ever thought possible. He had run through the pain and now, in his mind, it no longer existed. He was gasping for breath and his heart was racing. His face was pink, his hair matted down with sweat. It was pouring off him. He could see the man and the girl three quarters of the way down the hill, chasing after a cattle truck. They would never make it...

He became almost giddy with excitement. He raised his pistol and took careful aim.

Noonan and Anna raced blindly after the truck. But had it not been for the two lone cars that happened to pass along the road at the end of the track at that precise moment, the cattle truck would never have stopped, and Noonan and Anna would never have been allowed those few crucial seconds to close the gap and grab onto a rail on the back of the truck. No sooner had they grabbed it, the truck indicated left and disappeared down the road.

Behind them, the killer loosed off two shots from his pistol, but it was too late. The truck had disappeared.

The truck gathered speed along the road. Noonan and Anna lifted themselves over a hatch and rolled themselves into the back of the truck.

Noonan's body dropped into blackness. Anna landed next to him. There was a peculiar grunting sound coming from the half-light and the soft movement of little feet on wooden floorboards. Sunlight was streaming through two slats on both sides of the truck. Peering closer, Noonan could see that they were sharing the truck with animals of some kind. Lots of them... PIGS! Noonan sank to the floor and put his hand down.   It landed in something warm and comforting.   But it smelled intense.   Noonan suddenly realised... And then he immediately wanted to vomit.

"Oh no!" he murmured miserably. "Well... Shit."

Beside him Anna started to laugh.

Jarrett ran out onto the road, just catching sight of the truck as it disappeared round a corner.   The sound of its engine faded into nothing.   He shoved the pistol back into his pocket.

He was alone.   On a road, miles from anywhere.   A speck on the landscape. He had never had to work so hard to catch a quarry.   He had given everything he had on this day.   And still it had not been enough.   And he had got so close.

Jarrett dropped to his knees on the tarmac and leaned over, fighting back the phlegm and the bile that was rising in him. He looked up at the sky and realised suddenly how small he was in such a vast universe.

For the first time in his life, Jarrett felt tears welling up in his eyes.   And like a child, he wept.   And wept.

17

The Montagu Club, a Gentlemen's club founded in the nineteenth century, stood in an eight-storey town house not less than a five-minute walk from the Bank of England. The club itself was a social and business club, counting amongst its two hundred or so members certain sections of the aristocracy, various chairmen of the top merchant banks, and even the occasional Whitehall warrior. In accordance with the rules of the Gentlemen's clubs, some of which had been in place since the mid-nineteenth century, a strict dress code had been maintained down the decades. Suits were always worn, and women were not permitted on the premises. Some of the Gentlemen's clubs had relaxed this rule to the extent that some of them now boasted women among its members, but not the Montagu Club, which clung obstinately to old traditions.

Guarding these stringent traditions along with the privacy of the members was Smithson, often referred to affectionately by the members as "The Rottweiler", reflecting the pride and commitment he took in his role of keeping out any non-members or general undesirables. One thing that Smithson did not know however, was that the nickname that he took so much pride in - "The Rottweiler" – had been concocted by its members as a joke. For Smithson was no Rottweiler. It would have been too lavish a compliment to have likened him to a Pekinese. For the truth of the matter was that Smithson had rarely had to send anyone packing in all his years as the doorman of the Montagu Club. Such establishments were of no interest to anyone but its members. He was about to face his first real challenge in twenty-five years however, for he was about to cross swords with Tristan Head. And there could only be one outcome from a match like that.

At three o'clock that afternoon, Smithson could be found where he could always be found – dozing at his reception table at the end of the ornate, marble-floored reception area on the ground floor of the club. Just beyond Smithson's table was a wide, red-carpeted staircase leading up through the eight floors of the building. Smithson suddenly snapped to attention at the sharp sound of the *clack-clack-clack* of high heels on the hard, shiny marble floor. Striding purposefully towards him was Tristan Head and, alongside him, matching him step for step, was a tall, exceptionally beautiful woman, who Smithson took to be Head's personal secretary. He was half right.

Smithson felt immediately affronted. Head not only had the audacity to enter the building wearing a pale blue polo-neck sweater under an expensive sports jacket and a matching pair of trousers, but he had also brought a woman in with him. This deliberate flouting of etiquette was unforgivable. He would see to it that word got around. As if to confound and upset him even more, the woman was most appropriately dressed in a navy blue, pinstripe, three-piece ladies' suit. Underneath she wore a white blouse with a wide collar. He was about to find out that this was Anastasia, Head's wife, but he was not to know that this was in fact her preferred style of dress for visits to the city.

Tristan and the woman stepped up to Smithson's table.

"Ah, Smithson – my good man." There was a hint of mockery in Tristan's delivery that Smithson could not fail to detect. "I'd like you to meet my wife, Anastasia."

Smithson turned his attention to the woman who was smiling down on him with her large emerald eyes, sublimely disinterested. He rose to his feet.

"I really think, Sir, that..."

"How do you do," Anastasia greeted him with immaculate politeness.

"Er..." Smithson bumbled.

"I'm hoping you can help us. We're looking for Sir Lawrence Canning. I understand that he comes here regularly on Wednesday afternoons?"

"Sir, I must ask that you..."

"Sir Lawrence Canning – is he here?"

"Really, Mr Head, you know the rules   of   the..."

"Is he?"

Smithson's face was starting to assume a startling shade of pink. He failed to notice Anastasia step gracefully around the table, run her finger down the visitors' book until she found what she was

208

looking for, and then casually resume her position beside her husband.

"The Bannerman suite," she informed her husband.

"The Bannerman suite," Tristan repeated back to Smithson, with a nod and a smile. And at that they both turned and began to ascend the ornate staircase, leaving Smithson fuming and reeling in his own impotence.

"Doing a splendid job there, Smithson! Keep it up," Tristan called down as the *clack-clack-clack* of the high-heeled shoes rose to the upper floors of the building and faded into the oak panelling.

Tristan's information was watertight. Sir Lawrence sat perched in his favourite leather armchair with the latest edition of the Financial Times, a pipe protruding from his lips. He was in his mid-forties with tight grey curls and grey eyes that burned with intelligence. The Bannerman suite was a cavernous room that had once served as a banquet hall. Oak panelling rose two-thirds of the way up the high walls, which was then replaced by white masonry. There were four other gentlemen seated in the Bannerman suite, all wearing black, pinstripe suits, smoking, and rustling the newspapers on their laps. The smoke rose towards the ceiling where it hung like a fog on a damp autumnal morning.

Clack-clack-clack...

Sir Lawrence looked up from his newspaper at the unfamiliar sound that echoed around the vast room. Entering the suite at the far end was Tristan Head and alongside him was a woman he did not recognise. Immediately he was impressed by the woman's proud, aristocratic beauty. He should have been surprised to see a woman in the building but seeing as she was with Tristan he was not. As casually as he could, Sir Lawrence dropped the copy of the Financial Times down on the table next to his armchair, stood up, and started to saunter as purposefully as possible to the door at the other end of the room.

"Larry!"

The familiar voice of Tristan Head reached out across the room and seized him. Sir Lawrence slowly turned round, wearing the best look of surprise on his face that he could manage. Tristan and Anastasia were walking briskly towards him.

"Tristan!" he called out, investing as much pleasure into his voice as he could.

The other four elderly members of the club looked up from their papers and coughed their displeasure. Tristan and Anastasia walked straight up to him.

"I don't believe you've met, my wife, Anastasia. Anastasia, this is Sir Lawrence Canning. Sir Lawrence is on the board of the Builders and Constructional Workers Society. He probably knows more about the Construction industry in this country than anyone."

"How do you do?" Anastasia greeted him, not quite smiling. There was a slight hardness in her voice that Sir Lawrence did not understand. He looked into her face and was immediately dazzled by the largest pair of emerald eyes that he had ever seen on a woman's face. They sparkled at him with curiosity. He was aware of a fragrant aroma that came from her.

"I'm rather surprised to see you here, Tristan," continued Sir Lawrence.

"Are you, Larry? Are you surprised?" replied Tristan, with polite curiosity. Again, Sir Lawrence was caught off guard by Tristan's tone, and sensed trouble. "Now is there somewhere where we can speak privately?"

211

"Erm..."   Sir Lawrence made a gesture of looking at his watch.

"You needn't worry, Larry.   What I have to say won't take up much of your time."

"Very well.   We'll go to one of the ante-rooms."

Sir Lawrence led the way out of the Bannerman suite.   Tristan could feel four pairs of eyes staring through the back of his head in stern disapproval.   Sir Lawrence led them down a long, thin corridor covered from floor to ceiling in wood panelling.   Wall lamps were positioned along the wall at regular intervals, infusing the corridor in a warm, orange glow.   There were wooden doors set into the walls on both sides of the corridor with numbers on them.   Sir Lawrence stopped outside room 101 and indicated it with his head.   He gently opened the door and looked inside.   Then he beckoned Tristan and Anastasia in and closed the door.

There was a window high up just below the ceiling.   The wall on the left-hand side of the room was covered from floor to ceiling with books.   Two identical lamps to the ones in the corridor burned on the right-hand wall.   There was a shiny mahogany table in the centre of the small, square room with two leather chairs at both ends.

Anastasia took up a position at the table, leaning gently on it. She folded her arms and looked inquisitively at Sir Lawrence. Tristan slowly walked around the room, sniffing the air. He came back to Sir Lawrence and stood in front of him, his hands in his pockets. Sir Lawrence suddenly felt like he was in a police cell and was about to be questioned by two officers. He found himself deeply resenting it. His eyes looked over to Anastasia then slid back to Tristan, imploring him for privacy.

"I want Anastasia to stay and hear this," Tristan told him quietly.

"What do you want, Tristan?"

"The Maida Vale contract. The luxury apartments."

"Maida Vale?

Sir Lawrence cocked his head and gave a puzzled look.

"You know exactly what I'm talking about, Larry."

"Sit down, Larry," Anastasia softly ordered him.

"Now look here…"

"Sit down, Larry," Tristan repeated. "Please."

Sir Lawrence walked to the chair at the end of the table and sat down. His hands gently rubbed the arms of the chair. His expression was slightly petulant, but unworried. Only his hands gave him away.

"You're coming on heavy, Tristan. I'd be careful if I were you."

"Oh, relax, Larry, we're old pals." Tristan and Anastasia leaned against the table facing him. "That Maida Vale contract was mine, Larry. It was all fixed. But it ended up going to Mitchell. And Larry – you were the only other person at the planning stage who knew about it."

"Did you go to Mitchell with it?" Anastasia asked. Sir Lawrence turned away from her and stared at a spot on the ground a few feet away from him. "You did, didn't you, Larry?"

Sir Lawrence suddenly turned to Tristan, a note of anger edging into his voice. "I don't have to talk to you or your wife, Head." Tristan was unmoved. "I think this has gone far enough."

Sir Lawrence rose from the chair, but Anastasia gently pushed him back into it. "Sorry, Larry," she chided him. "But we really need to know. You see, it's the third time we've lost a contract. And we're not losing any more." She looked at Tristan. "I think he wants to tell us."

"Look, Larry, it's not you we're after, it's Mitchell. We can keep you out of this," Tristan told him.

Anastasia reached into her small handbag and took out a packet of Dunhill cigarettes. She flipped one into her mouth, took out a lighter and lit it. She extended the packet to Tristan, who quickly shook his head.

"Why did you do it, Larry? Why did you sell me out to Mitchell? Was it fear? Money? Old loyalties?" Tristan continued.

"Or has he got something on you?" asked Anastasia.

"I was always straight with you, Larry. Now I'm asking you to be straight with me. I can't undo what's already gone down. But I can stop it happening again."

"And, who knows?" Anastasia picked it up. "You deal with us and we could end up paying you a lot more than Mitchell."

"You owe me, Larry," Tristan concluded.

"You're wasting your time, Head," Sir Lawrence said after a pause. "I've got nothing to tell you."

"Well, I'm sorry to hear that, Larry," Tristan said softly. He paused before continuing carefully. "By the way, do you remember Anna, Larry? Anna Raven?"

Sir Larry looked at him oddly.

"She disappeared nine months ago," Tristan continued. "But you know all about that, don't you?"

"Mitchell's wife?" A look of mild panic flashed across his face. "So, they were having marital problems. Doesn't everyone? What does that have to do with me? Or you?"

"Well, it's just that before she disappeared, she was working with the police. Did you know that, Larry? Did you know that she was putting evidence together against her husband? Evidence that never saw the light of day. Evidence that's still in a safe place."

"And a good friend of ours is with the girl right now," Anastasia continued, leaning into Sir Lawrence. "We're on the point of getting that evidence. And when we do, Mitchell will go away for a long time."

"And so could you," said Tristan softly. "Unless you tell us what you know."

"Evidence, what are you talking about?" Sir Larry shook his head in mock disbelief.

"I wouldn't lie to you, Larry."

Tristan rose to his full height and looked down at him. Anastasia took a long pull on her cigarette and blew the smoke over Sir Lawrence's head. They waited.

Finally, Tristan said, "OK, if that's how you want it. I'll see you in court, Larry." Tristan and Anastasia walked towards the door.

"Wait."

The voice was suddenly imploring, defeated. Tristan and Anastasia stopped and turned.

"Look - I'm sorry you lost the contracts, Head, but trust me, it would have happened anyway. Mitchell's connections go all the way to the top."

Anastasia walked back to him. "Go on, Larry."

He shook his head. "There's not much I can tell you. But you're both in way over your heads. I shouldn't even be telling you anything."

Tristan and Anastasia stood on either side of him.

"Keep talking, Larry," Tristan ordered.

"You remember Fox?"

"The accountant? Died in a boating accident if I recall correctly."

"He was a master yachtsman, for God's sake! He took part in round the world races. Do you think that sort of thing happens to those kinds of people every day?"

Tristan and Anastasia shared a look. Anastasia felt her heart beginning to beat faster.

"And Bowen. And Lahaise."

"They started up around the same time as me." Tristan's mind was racing. "But Bowen had a weak heart! He was always on borrowed time."

"Believe me, they got to both of them."

"They?" prompted Anastasia.

"Mitchell's got someone in Scotland Yard on his payroll. And there's someone else too, someone even higher up, in Government. They've been receiving money from Mitchell's building operations to finance their own operations abroad. Not even I'm supposed to know about it. If that ever got out..."

"Do you know their names, Larry?" Tristan asked.

"I don't and nor do I want to."

"And you," Tristan continued. "He's had you in his pocket, Larry, all this time. For God's sake, why did you do it?"

Sir Lawrence turned his head down and stared at the carpet again, his eyes seeing nothing.

"I've been having some financial difficulties. People I owe money to. Not the sort of people you can keep waiting. And then there was the divorce. It seemed the only way out."

Sir Lawrence's mouthed moved but no more words came out. He just shook his head once and that was it. Then he turned back to Tristan.

"You understand?"

Tristan leaned in. "Well done, Larry." He patted him gently on the shoulder. Anastasia extinguished her cigarette in a silver ashtray. Then they turned and walked briskly out of the room, leaving Sir Larry slumped in his chair, like a condemned man.

Tristan and Anastasia walked briskly past Smithson on the way out again. Understandably, his head was down, and he avoided eye contact with them completely. Tristan knew that he would be blackballed from the club for his flagrant breach of the rules, but he didn't care. He had no further use for the club in any case.

18

Sir Lawrence arrived back at his mews house in Kensington at half past six. He kicked his shoes off without picking them up and putting them next to each other. He stepped over the pile of envelopes spread across his doormat without even noticing them. He immediately went straight through to his kitchen, loosening his tie as he did so and discarding it on the hall carpet. Once in the kitchen, he shrugged his way clumsily out of his suit jacket and threw it carelessly over one of the kitchen chairs. Such a spreading of mess was wildly out of character for Sir Lawrence Canning. On any other day he would have fastidiously put his shoes together and hung his coat up. Every suit he owned had its own hanger and his shoes had their own special spot on the wooden rack. But this evening Sir Lawrence was rattled and anxious. He could not remember feeling like this for a long time. His life was one of calm order and precision, a life of casual privilege, and he had always felt secure, protected within it. But this afternoon he had crossed a line. He had told Tristan Head too much.

Sir Lawrence looked around the kitchen and suddenly wondered why he had gone in there. What he needed was in the drawing room – and he was going to need plenty of it to calm his nerves.

Ten minutes later, he was sunk low in the armchair of his perfectly ordered drawing room, nervously clutching a glass of red wine. The photographs of his wife and two young sons smiled benignly back at him from the other side of the room, but his eyes barely focussed on them. It had been only two years, but it now seemed like another existence entirely. He wondered for a second what they were all doing right now and if they were all happy. How was she managing with them on her own? *Was* she in fact still on her own? Then the anxiety kicked in again and he instantly forgot them. His mind focussed on Tristan and his wife. He had *had* to answer Tristan's questions. Tristan was getting closer to the evidence and he knew that he would not stop until he had found it. And he saw no reason to go down with the ship. No-one could possibly ever know what had been discussed in that little room.   Could they?

He remained in that armchair for the next hour.   By this point he had managed to dampen his nerves in four glasses of red wine.   Then the doorbell harshly screamed at him.   He jerked in his armchair, shocked.   Who was that?   He could not face talking to anyone right now. He wanted them to go the hell away and leave him alone.   But the lights were all on.   It was obvious he was at home.   But who would be calling at this time?   There was one possibility that was so appalling that he could hardly bear to think about it. Shakily putting his glass down on the table next to him, Sir Lawrence got to his feet and walked to the front door.   He opened it.   Instantly, Sir Lawrence's heart plummeted inside him.

Standing outside on the rain-soaked street with a savage grin on his face was Lee Mitchell.   Next to him was a younger man in his early thirties.   The expression on his face was half-smile and half-sneer.   He looked brash, cocky but capable.   Both men wore suits underneath their raincoats.

"Good evening, Larry!"   Mitchell was being far too jocular.   It made Sir

Lawrence feel uneasy and suspicious. "I hope it's not an inconvenient time, but we do need to talk. Can we come in?" He felt the younger man's eyes probing him keenly.

"Er..." Sir Lawrence stumbled for a moment.

"Nice mews! I could do with one of these myself. Very homely."

"Yes, yes, it erm..." Sir Lawrence was bumbling, and he knew it. "It does me very nicely."

"It's getting a bit wet out here," Mitchell prompted him.

"Oh, yes – come in."

Sir Lawrence stood to one side and the two men brushed past him, striding down the corridor as if they already owned the place. Mitchell reached the drawing room door and pointed.

"In here, is it?" His loud voice bounced off the walls and straight back at Sir Lawrence.

"Yes, do go in."

They did so, followed by Sir Lawrence. Without waiting to be invited, both men sat down on the settee, the younger man on the sofa, Mitchell in the other armchair. Mitchell spotted the wine on the table and nodded to it.

"You must have been expecting us, Larry! If you don't mind, we wouldn't say no."

"I'll just fetch a couple of glasses," Sir Lawrence mumbled quietly. He quickly excused himself. Mitchell looked around the drawing room.

"You see the rewards that come from working for the right people, Remy. Look around. This could be yours one day. In fact, this very one could be on the market very soon."

Remy said nothing, just looked at Mitchell and nodded once. At that moment Sir Lawrence came back in with two red wines. He handed them to his guests and took his usual seat by the table.

"Oh, I don't think you've met my er, business partner, Remy," Mitchell remarked. "Remy - meet Sir Lawrence Canning. One of my most trusted and loyal associates."

Sir Lawrence could not fail to detect the nasty undercurrent in Mitchell's voice when he said this. Remy just nodded again, without expression. Sir Lawrence smiled quickly. Mitchell took a delicate sip of the red wine. He let it go down and then let out a slow, satisfied "Aaahh..." He smiled warmly at Sir Lawrence.

"Tell me, Larry, have you been seeing much of Tristan Head lately?" Mitchell's open, friendly smile did not waver.

"What's this all about, Mitchell?"

Remy leaned forward slightly.

"Well, it has come to my attention that my old sparring partner, Tristan Head, made rather a scene this afternoon up at the Montagu. Even took his wife in there with him. They don't like that sort of thing, do they?" A smile spread across his face like an alligator. "I, er, gather he was looking for you. Now, would our information be correct?"

"He, er..."

Mitchell raised an eyebrow.

"He stayed for a few minutes and left. There wasn't much I could help him with. He seemed to be on the wrong end of the stick."

"That sounds like my boy, Tristan. What did you talk about?" Sir Lawrence looked uneasily from one man to the other. Mitchell continued in his most reasonable tone. "I don't mean to pry, Larry, but you see, you and I have a special relationship. And we trust each other with some extremely valuable secrets. Don't we?"

Sir Lawrence nodded numbly.

"So, you would understand my being curious." Mitchell put his glass down. "What did you talk about, Larry?"

Sir Lawrence was silent.

"Do you know what I love about red wine, Larry?" Mitchell suddenly asked. "It makes one very chatty."

At this, Remy swiftly got to his feet and moved over to Sir Lawrence's side.

Quietly Mitchell said, "Drink up, Larry."

Remy leaned over and picked up the glass, putting it to Sir Lawrence's lips.

"Go on," ordered Remy in a tough, quiet voice. "Down the hatch, old son." Suddenly with his left hand, he pulled Sir Lawrence's head back and started to pour the liquid down his throat. Sir Lawrence spluttered and gurgled, the wine gushing out of his throat and down his shirt.

"Bottoms up," Mitchell added, settling back in the armchair, clasping his fingers together and watching the spectacle as if he were a child at a cinema watching a particularly exciting film.

Don Wiseman and his wife Maisie ambled over the crest of the hill at half past seven and back towards Rectory Farm, which they owned. It was now pitch-black outside, and the rain had started again, but they walked this track practically every day and knew virtually every pothole. They had been one of the last to leave the celebrations in the small hamlet, having helped clear up. Don had overdone it again on the cider, a particular weakness of his, and had become boisterous and randy as a result, but Maisie was used to this and had no problem overlooking such over-indulgences. Overall, though, everyone had gone home happy and in good spirits, despite the rather unpleasant episode with the three strangers earlier in the afternoon. It seemed that it was unwise to trust anyone outside of the hamlet. There would always be trouble.

Don made it to the front door first and fumbled with the key. He felt around in the dark for the light switch and turned it on. He shrugged himself out of his overcoat and hung it up. Then he staggered into the kitchen, his face still warm, ruddy, and flush from the excitement of the day and the effects of the cider. He turned the light on. And the warmth instantly left his face.

Sitting at the kitchen table was a stranger. His eyes were black and empty. His face carried no interest, no expression.

His hair was jet black and hung messily over his ears. An ugly red scar protruded under his lower lip. He devoured Don Wiseman with his stare. Don found himself unable to move, unable to take his eyes away. He remembered his face from earlier in the afternoon. A face he had hoped never to see again. The stranger had a gun in his right hand which was pointing at Don's stomach. The hand that held it was rock-steady.

At that moment, Maisie came stumbling into the kitchen, calling out, "Oh Don, I..." Then she gasped in shock when she saw the stranger sitting at their table. The stranger did not take his eyes off Don. Maisie, always the more forceful and dominant of the two, was the first to speak.

"What is this? Who are you? What do you want?" she rasped. She could not keep the quiver out of her voice on the last question.

The stranger waited a beat before replying in a reedy whisper.

"I want food. I want you to fix up my thigh. And when you've done all that, I want you to tell me where that truck was going that left here this afternoon. And don't lie to me – because if you do, I'll know. I can tell. And I'll kill you for it."

Don and Maisie Wiseman stared back at the stranger, unable to respond.

At ten to nine that evening, Tristan's Range Rover swept into the car park of The Wheatsheaf on The Green. It was a long, white building with a rural tinge, a convenient watering hole for all the stockbrokers and chartered accountants that lived nearby either in Esher or Hinchley Wood.

It was busy at that time of the evening, but Tristan was lucky to arrive just as a Hillman Avenger was leaving. Tristan swiftly swept into the parking space. A second later, he disembarked with Anastasia, who was now wearing a sheepskin overcoat. Her hair was tied back in a bun. Tristan was wearing a heavy, black leather overcoat. They strode into the pub and looked around.

Detective Inspector Ronnie Spooner of Scotland Yard had arrived ahead of them and had found a table in a quiet alcove. He clapped eyes on Tristan and nodded. Tristan raised his hand in greeting before making his way to the bar.

A young barmaid wearing a blouse that left nothing to the imagination was serving behind the bar. He had to wait five minutes before the young barmaid eventually turned to meet them.

"A white wine and a G&T, please."

"White wine and G&T?"

"That's right."

"Coming right up, my darling."

Tristan found it strange being referred to in such a way by a girl young enough to be his daughter. He smiled to himself. The drinks came, Tristan paid for them, and they made their way to the alcove. Tristan and Anastasia sat down opposite Spooner.

"Thank you for meeting me, Ronnie."

"Well, we Sandhurst boys have to stick together." He had a pint of ale in a tall glass and he took a swig from it. "Alright, Tristan. What have you got for me?"

Tristan started to tell him everything, starting with the telephone call he had received from Noonan the previous day, ending with the unidentified Scotland Yard man in Mitchell's pocket, and the conspiracy that ran all the way into the Government.

Spooner listened and nodded. Ronnie Spooner had a tough, military-like face. He wore a trench coat over a grey suit, had a thick black moustache, broad shoulders and hard, watchful eyes that seemed to look right through a man and know instinctively when he was lying. The tip of his moustache imperceptibly twitched.

"Hmm…" He stared thoughtfully into his ale. "Can you give me the name of your friend?"

"Sorry, Ronnie. But if I can get that evidence, it's yours."

"I see." Spooner sat and thought for a few seconds. Then he reached into his inside jacket pocket and pulled out a black and white photograph.

"The information you asked for," he said, handing over the photograph. The face of the man in the picture immediately sent a chill down Tristan's spine. It was a blow-up of a monochrome passport photograph. The man wore a black leather jacket and stared with a lethargic deadliness right into the lens. His black eyes seemed to bore into Tristan's. He briefly examined the photograph then quickly handed it back to Spooner, not wishing to look at the frightening face any longer, convinced that he could never forget it for as long as he lived.

"Jarrett – James Michael. Former serviceman," Spooner informed him. "He was in Northern Ireland until he was dishonourably discharged from the forces. Now he works for money. We know he's an associate of Mitchell's."

"Jarrett," Tristan repeated, committing the name to memory. He showed the photograph to Anastasia, who just nodded. He handed the photograph back to Spooner, who slipped it back into his pocket. He then carefully looked over all the other people in the place. His eyes grew wary and distrustful.

"Who else knows about all this?"

"Just you."

He then turned slowly to Tristan and spoke to him in a soft but unyielding voice. His eyes hardened. "Good. Because you just forget what you heard about the Government being involved with Mitchell. You just stay away from that, you understand?"

His eyes bore into Tristan's like twin drills. Tristan finally nodded.

"OK, Ronnie. I understand."

"Because if it ever gets out that we know, I could end up a discredited ex-policeman.   And you two could end up very quickly in a mortuary."

19

       Earlier that day, Noonan and Anna had found their long, twisting journey in the back of the pig truck to be thoroughly uncomfortable. All they could see through the small partition above the half-door was the varying cloud formations in the sky and the occasional peak of a hill jutting into view. The truck seemed to shift to the left, to the right, forever meandering through the countryside. Meanwhile Noonan and Anna found themselves the subjects of never-ending fascination for the pigs, who continually sniffed around their feet, grunting in what could have been satisfaction or protest, it was hard to tell, and occasionally prodding them with their noses. Noonan and Anna pressed themselves up against the driver's cabin as the pigs besieged them. Noonan had never had any love for pigs. They seemed comically ugly creatures to him and they made filthy noises. His forced sojourn with them in the back of the truck was doing nothing to further endear them to him. The continual grunting and burping noises were revolting. And the smell! He found a nearby clump of straw on which he was able to wipe the dirt off his hand. Anna, on the other hand, seemed to be finding the appalling creatures quite delightful. She was watching Noonan's continuing unease with a certain amount of amusement. Occasionally, she would look at him and chuckle. Five minutes after they had settled down, a tiny piglet had leapt up into her arms.

"Awww..." She had crowed affectionately at it. "Hello, my darling. I think I'm going to call you Tom." She turned to him, laughing as he shifted miserably away from the creature. It lifted its ugly little snout to sniff cautiously at him. One other little piglet seemed to catch Noonan's eye as it made its way towards him from the back of the truck. It had a splash of orange across its back that made it distinguishable from the others. As the other pigs and piglets milled around aimlessly, this little piglet seemed to move purposefully and fearlessly towards Noonan, its little snout sniffing ahead, sniffing out Noonan. Noonan saw it coming, cutting a straight path towards him. He squirmed. The little piglet got to him and, like little Tom in Anna's arms, leapt up into Noonan's arms.

"Ahhh!" he gasped in horror. "Get off me! Get away!"

He tried to set the piglet down, but the piglet had no intention of going anywhere. It just turned round and fixed Noonan with a decisive look, its snout making its preliminary evaluation.

"Looks like I'm stuck with you, eh?" Noonan said to the piglet, who plainly was not interested in conversation. Instead, it just turned its back on Noonan and pointed its backside up at his face.

"Don't you even think about it," warned Noonan severely. He turned to Anna, a worried look on his face. "What am I supposed to call it? Anna?"

Anna was laughing. She indicated the splash of orange on the piglet's back. "Why not? She's a little redhead, sort of like me. And like me, she never takes no for an answer." She looked down at Noonan's piglet and stroked its head. "You're a strong-willed little girl, aren't you? But be careful – he's my man, and don't you forget it."

"I won't have the two of you fighting over me," Noonan told her.

"You know, you surprise me, Noonan," she replied. "A tough man like you – frightened of these little piglets."

"I'm not frightened of them, I just don't like them," Noonan replied indignantly.

"Give them time," Anna replied. "You'll learn to love them."

The truck continued its journey. Noonan and Anna spent the next part of it huddling their piglets to their chests and stroking them. As Anna had told him, Noonan had relaxed with the piglet and an understanding was starting to develop between them, if not an outright affection. By this point, the rest of the pigs had decided that the two imposters were not worth wasting any further time on and had trundled to the back of the truck and left them to it.

"You know, Noonan," Anna began, "when this is all over, if we're still alive, we should maybe get ourselves a farm. An animal farm, I mean. Not crops or that sort of thing but raise little piglets like these. It would be our farm. We could pay some labourers to help us with the work. We'd be able to get away from it all. Don't you ever think about that sort of thing?"

"Farming?" Noonan had in fact never thought about farming. He shook his head and looked puzzled.

"Why not?"

"I don't know," Noonan shook his head.

"You've got to settle down sometime, Noonan," Anna said to him. "Everyone has to. We've still got a chance, you know."

"To raise piglets?"

She nodded and shrugged.

"And what happens to the piglets? They get taken away and slaughtered. And then they become food. And then you raise more piglets. Same things happen to them in time. And that's just the way it goes." He paused. "That's the way it is everywhere."

"I know," Anna said. "What I'm saying is, I'm not going to let this maniac kill either of us. I want us to survive and live a life."

Noonan just turned to her and smiled. He leant over to her and kissed her on the forehead. They were silent for a few moments. Then Anna spoke again.

"Noonan. If we go to the police, they'll find this man and put him away. Won't they?"

"Well, it's my guess that Mitchell's got someone highly placed within the police force, someone working with him. How else would he have known a year ago that you working with the police to put him away? No, I don't think the police are the answer. When it comes to it, we may have to deal with him ourselves."

"You mean kill him?"

"When it comes down to it, he won't hesitate to kill us, not for a second. And neither will I. So, neither must you if you get your chance."

"Noonan, he's got one handgun at least. What have we got?"

"This is farming country. There's no shortage of shotguns out here. You may have to learn to use one."

"I'll do whatever I have to do," Anna told him decisively. Noonan knew she meant it.

"That's good," Noonan replied. "Just don't get to like it too much, that's all."

"Is there any danger of that?" Anna replied.

Noonan reached out his hand and Anna took it. The piglets nestled comfortably into Noonan and Anna's chests and closed their eyes, their little chests throbbing with life. Noonan squeezed Anna's hand gently and kept holding it.

The truck continued along its way as the skies began to darken outside.

It was dusk by the time the truck started to climb a steep hill, finally stopping at the top. They had been in the truck for over an hour. The pigs suddenly stopped moving, sensing that they had reached the end of their journey. The piglets, Tom, and Anna stayed where they were in the arms of Noonan and Anna. Voices could be heard outside. Noonan listened. There were three voices at least, all male. The dominant voice belonged to an older man with a strong welsh accent. The other two voices sounded very much younger, possibly belonging to young men in their early twenties. The older voice clearly belonged to the man in charge. It was a gruff voice and carried the weight of authority with it. Noonan began to wonder what kind of a reception they would get when they finally got out of the truck.

"Right! Let's get those little bastards out!" barked the gruff, welsh voice.

Noonan heard the bolts being pulled back and the half-door being pulled down. It was lowered to the ground to become a ramp for the pigs to be ushered out. A young, lanky figure climbed up into the truck and started to usher the pigs out and onto the ramp. Long, blond, feminine hair flowed down his back. For a while, the young lad was so preoccupied with his work that he failed to notice Noonan and Anna lurking at the back of the truck. Then he turned and spotted them. He stopped in his tracks.

"Mr Burton?" he called out.

Noonan and Anna rose to their feet but said nothing.

"Mr Burton?" he called out again, raising his voice now.

The gruff welsh voice answered with a degree of impatience.

"What is it, laddie?"

The young lad rose to his fullest height and looked disapprovingly down at Noonan and Anna.

"Take it easy, son, we can explain everything," Noonan tried to reassure him.

"Two strangers in the back of the truck here," continued the young lad. "Hey, put those piglets down, they don't belong to you!" he suddenly shouted at them, looking, and feeling personally affronted. He had a strong west country accent. Noonan and Anna kept hold of the piglets. Then the owner of the gruff, authoritative Welsh voice stepped up into the truck and stood glowering at Noonan and Anna. Noonan could only see his silhouette but could nevertheless still see his eyes blazing furiously at them. He was a thick, heavy set man with long hair covering his ears.

"Right, you two!" he barked at them. "Get out of there, let's have a good look at you!"

Noonan and Anna edged carefully forward. The piglets had all been led out of the truck by now. The gruff Welshman and the younger lad stepped backwards onto the ramp and walked to the ground. Noonan and Anna stood at the edge of the van, looking down at the three men. The third man was much smaller in size, with short black hair and a kind, gentle face. He looked somewhat bewildered.

"All the way down, come on!" ordered the Welshman ferociously. He started to beckon them with both his hands. Noonan and Anna did as they were instructed and stepped to the ground. Noonan suddenly felt very foolish with

Anna the piglet still in his arms. The driver of the truck opened his door and came around to see what the shouting was all about. He had long, curly black hair and was wearing a sheepskin waistcoat and a pair of jeans. He had a gypsy look about him.

"What's going on?" he asked, taking in the scene around him. He looked suspiciously at Anna and Noonan. "And who are they?"

"That's what we're going to find out," snarled the Welshman. He eyed Noonan with suspicion. "Aren't we?"

"You mean they've been travelling in the back of my truck all this time?"

"Don't worry, Reuben. We'll find out soon enough." The voice continued to lash out at them. "You put those piglets down!"

Noonan and Anna did as they were told. Tom and Anna scuttled away to join their comrades, grunting, and burping as they did so.

"Trying to steal my stock, eh?" growled the Welshman. "You thought you'd get away with it, I suppose? Trying your luck…"

Noonan looked hard at the Welshman. It was clearly his intention to intimidate them into submission and possibly a confession. It was a tough, fierce, fighting man's face. Noonan had seen many faces like it in his life, from his time in the army and then after. But this man's face was tougher than most. This was the face of a man who controlled his farm, his own fiefdom, with absolute authority. The lines on his face were like battle scars accumulated over the years. Noonan understood this man instantly. He was a born fighter, a natural survivor. Noonan was going to have trouble with him. He meant to show that he was not afraid of him and would not be intimidated. He walked slowly towards him.

"Now you listen to me..." he started, his voice low, icy, and controlled. He noticed the Welshman's arms come apart and his fists lock together. Fury burned in his pale green eyes. His nostrils flared. "We're not here to steal your pigs. And the back of that filthy truck is the last place either of us wanted to be. But we're tired and we're in a lot of trouble right now. I don't need any more of it. You get me?"

Noonan continued looking at the face. It was the face of a wrestler or a prize fighter. The nose looked slightly broken.

The skin looked ravaged with the passing of the hard years and an enthusiastic indulgence in alcohol. Noonan could smell it on his breath. Anna came up and stood beside Noonan. She put her hand on his arm. The other three men closed ranks behind the Welshman. Noonan looked at the four men. If it came down to it, he was going to have to take all four of them. But he did not want to do this. The three young men behind the gruff Welshmen had fresh, innocent faces and probably knew nothing about fighting. They presented no challenge. From the look of them, Anna could probably take them. So, it would be between him and the Welshman. Noonan knew he could take him easily. The Welshman was about twenty years older and out of shape. But Noonan sensed that while this man might go down, he would keep getting back up again. There was no beating a man like this. Noonan suddenly felt weary and realised how little he wanted this senseless fight to happen.

"Yes, I'd say you were indeed in a lot of trouble right now," growled the Welshman. "Seth. Run inside, get the police over here right now."

The tall lad with the long blond hair started to run towards a vast, sturdy looking farmhouse several yards further down the drive.

"Wait!" called Noonan.

Seth froze in mid-run and turned back, his leg hovering in mid-air.

"Why are you afraid of the police? Got something to hide, have you?" The Welshman's eyes glittered fiercely.

"We don't have anything to hide. But the police can't help us. I don't expect you to believe me, but we've been on the run for three days. There's a man out there who wants to kill us. This afternoon he nearly succeeded. We're tired and we need help. Trust me, I'm not lying."

The Welshman studied Noonan carefully. Then slowly he nodded. When he spoke again, his voice was suddenly quiet, measured and even.

"I'll be the judge of whether or not you're lying. OK, you can come in and have supper with us for now. But if you turn out to be any kind of trouble, I'll take you in to the police myself. You understand?"

Noonan nodded. "I understand. And thank you."

"For what it's worth," continued the Welshman, "I'm leaning towards believing you. I've had to sort out a few troublemakers and thieves in my time. You get to know a look, a smell. And neither of you look or smell like troublemakers." The Welshness in his voice came out even more strongly now that he was speaking quietly. Then he suddenly smiled, and his face was utterly transformed. Suddenly it was the warmest, most delightful face that Noonan had seen in a long time, full of life, experience, and character. Noonan found himself smiling back, feeling an immediate connection with the man. For the first time in three days, he felt that they may have found an ally.

"Are you hungry?" the Welshman asked.

Noonan turned to Anna. She nodded. Noonan turned back to the Welshman and nodded too.

"Seth will whip up something for you. My name's Burton. Come along now." Burton led Noonan and Anna into the farmhouse, Seth and Jacko following behind them. Reuben stayed behind to direct the pigs into a nearby pen to join another vast community. He opened the wooden gate and with a chorus of grunts and burps, the pigs, and piglets, occasionally tripping over each other, crashed their way into the pen.

"In you go then, my little darlings," he softly cooed to them with his soft west country burr, a winsome smile on his face. Satisfied that they were all in, Reuben locked the gate and jogged back to the truck.   He jumped into the cabin and reversed it backwards so that it was neatly parked in a nearby courtyard a little way from the farmhouse.   Reuben jumped out again, locked the driver's door, shoved the bunch of keys into the pocket of his jeans and jogged into the farmhouse to join the others.

20

Burton led Noonan and Anna down a hall with a low ceiling. The place was dusty and smelled ever so faintly of cat urine. There was a collection of anoraks and wet weather clothes hanging on some hooks down the right-hand wall. Burton beckoned to them to remove their overcoats and hang them up, which they did. There was a door at the end on the left and this led into a spacious kitchen. There was a large wooden table in the centre of the room with four wooden chairs at each side. The floor was covered with red tiles and black beams stretched across a low ceiling. There was a stove, a cooker and a basin at the far end of the room. Burton beckoned them to sit down. He sat down at the head of the table which Noonan assumed was his usual seat. Noonan and Anna sat side by side of him. Burton leaned forward, placing his arms firmly on the table. He looked from one to the other.

"Now, why don't you tell me all about it?"

It took twenty minutes to describe their flight from Denby and everything that had happened to them up to the moment that the half-door of the pig truck had been opened and Burton had discovered them stowing away there. Anna had taken over the part of the story that had involved her flight from her husband, her attempt to start a new life in Denby, up to the point when Noonan had saved her from Mitchell's thugs in the church. Then it had been back to Noonan. The only part of the story that Noonan omitted was his history before he had arrived in Denby. As far as Burton was concerned, he was a drifter who had happened to be in the right place at the right time, which was in fact true.

At the end of it, Burton sat slowly back in his chair, locked his fingers together and pressed them against his chin. He exhaled loudly and slowly, his eyes swivelling up to the ceiling. After a few seconds he looked back at Noonan and Anna. The fading light from the window illuminated his grey hair and beard.

"I could arrange for you to see the local Chief Inspector of police, Owen

251

Kilgariff," he mused in his Welsh accent. "I know him rather well, actually. This is the sort of small community where everyone is known to each other. He'd be able to help. You'd be safe with him. Would you like me to do that?"

Anna turned to Noonan. "Well..." she hesitated.

"It would be a good idea, Anna," Noonan advised her. "Then you'd be safe."

"But what about you?"

"What about me?"

"Would you come too?"

"I doubt it," he replied, shaking his head.

"Then I won't go," she told him affirmatively.

She turned back to Burton, who was now looking at Noonan slightly warily.

"Are you in trouble with the police or something?" Burton wanted to know.

"I'm not a criminal," Noonan answered. "I just have my own reasons for avoiding the police."

Burton gave him a hard look. "If you turn out to be any kind of trouble, I'll fix you, my boy," he rumbled with a hint of menace.

"You'll have no trouble. You have my word," Noonan assured him.

"I hope so. Because I'm putting my trust in you." He turned back to Anna. "Well, it's up to you really," he continued in a lighter, more avuncular manner. "If you change your mind, let me know."

A hooting sound came from one wall of the room. Noonan turned. A cuckoo clock on the wall above the oven was announcing that it was six o'clock. Almost as though they had been drilled, the three young men walked into the kitchen at that moment, laughing at a shared joke.

"Ah, here comes the rabble," Burton sighed. "I think it's about time I introduced you to my workforce and extended family." The three young men fanned out and stood in front of them. The thin boy with the long blond hair and the angelic face stood to the left. He was dressed in jeans and a baggy sweater. Burton pointed to him. "This lad here is Seth." He then pointed to the boy in the middle, who was clearly the youngest and looked no older than eighteen years of age. He had short, tidy black hair and a kind, innocent face. "This one here is Jacko. And finally, we have..." he pointed to the long, curly haired man in the sheepskin waistcoat, who looked slightly older.

"Reuben?" Noonan prompted him.

"That's right, Reuben," Burton confirmed, then turned to Noonan and Anna. "Perhaps you'd like to make your own introductions."

"Anna Raven." Anna smiled warmly at the three boys, who stood there, slightly goggle-eyed at the prospect of having such a young and beautiful woman sharing their kitchen, an obviously rare privilege.

"Tom Noonan." Noonan nodded slightly. They all looked at him, mumbling their greetings. Noonan could see them sizing him up, making their own assessments of the man who they clearly took to be her boyfriend. Reuben seemed the most perturbed at the presence of the two strangers at their kitchen table and shot a questioning look at Burton. Burton picked up on this.

"It's OK, Reuben," he assured him. "Our friends appear to have run into a spot of trouble. We're going to provide them with shelter for a bit."

"What kind of trouble are you in?" Reuben asked Noonan with suspicion.

"I'm sure Mr Noonan will tell you in good time – if that's what he wants to do," answered Burton. Reuben nodded, backing down. Burton turned back to

Noonan and Anna. "And I'm Richard Burton."

Noonan's face remained stoic, but Burton caught Anna's eyes sparkling in recognition of the name.

"Yes, yes, I know, I've heard all the jokes." Burton rumbled amiably. He pointed over to Seth. "Seth here is our cook. What are you making for us tonight, Seth?"

"Sausage casserole," Seth replied, casting his eyes downwards.

"Can I help at all?" Anna asked, her eyes lighting up. All eyes turned to her. "I enjoy cooking."

Seth looked quizzically at her.

"Why not? We all muck in around here as best we can," answered Burton. "And I've no doubt that Seth would appreciate an extra pair of hands. Isn't that so, Seth?"

"Yes, Mr Burton," Seth responded automatically.

Anna jumped up and moved towards the oven, saying as she went, "I won't get in the way." She began to speak with Seth as he opened cupboards and drawers to prepare for the meal. Reuben and Jacko went and sat on a long bench by the window, facing each other. Reuben reached over to the window and picked up a pack of cards. He fanned them with his thumb, cut them impressively and started to deal. Noonan watched them with mild interest. He could imagine that for them this was a daily ritual while waiting for supper to be served. They became totally absorbed in the game, oblivious to everything that was going on around them. Noonan and Burton were left together.

"They're good lads," Burton told him.

"How did you find them?" Noonan asked.

"Oh, they found me," he replied. "They were without families, without a home. So, I took them in and gave them one. I give them work and a way of life. They know they can leave whenever they like, but they never do. They seem to like it here. And why not? They're good workers and I pay a fair rate."

"They just turned up on your doorstep?"

"More or less," confirmed Burton. "There are plenty of them about, I can tell you. It's a shame." Burton shook his head and reached across for a bottle of malt whisky. He filled a glass. "Will you join me?"

Noonan raised a hand and shook his head. "Well, now you've got five. I have to tell you though; I know nothing about pig farming."

"Oh, you'll learn quick enough."

"I was a mechanic in the army."

"That could be useful. A couple of my vehicles need repairs, and my usual man won't be available for a fortnight."

Burton began to relate his story as Noonan watched Anna and Seth working together. Anna was slicing onions and carrots while Seth prepared the sausages. Noonan tuned into Burton's story and caught the bullet points. He had bought the farm twenty-five years previously with his wife; she had died ten years later giving birth to a son, who had then died several days later; the years had been hard, but he had kept going and the farm was now doing good business; the previous ten years had seen a steady increase in revenue and the farm could now provide some comfort. Noonan imagined that the hard knocks that Mr Burton had had to face would have been enough to finish off most men, but every time Burton had come back fighting, and if he did not always win, he had certainly always managed to stay in the game. There was tragedy in his story but there was also triumph. Noonan hoped that Burton would not enquire too deeply into his history and mercifully he did not.

It took an hour for the sausage casserole to be prepared and when it came, along with the mashed potatoes and runner beans, it was piping hot and delicious. Two more chairs were found for Noonan and Anna so that they could all fit round the table. Everyone made a point of congratulating Anna and Seth on the splendid meal. The discussion at the table centred around the lads' fetish for motorcycles (a four-way conversation that Noonan happily contributed to), the possibility of taking a drive to the nearest cinema to see the latest releases (thirty miles away, and usually a bi-annual outing) and, of course, the pigs. Reuben and Seth had mentioned that they were saving up to buy motorbikes and Noonan offered to advise in any way he could. Towards the end of the meal, Noonan had begun to worry about his scheduled call to Tristan, which he had not been able to make. He knew Tristan would be expecting this.

"Would you mind if I made a phone call after supper?" Noonan asked Burton during a convenient break in their conversation. "It's very important."

"There's a phone in the lounge. You can use that. You can speak privately there; the lads usually go to their rooms after supper."

It was half past eight when supper finally wound down. Noonan and Anna offered to clear the table and wash up, which the lads were grateful for as it meant they could get away. Noonan was to discover that meals took up a major part of the evening in this establishment. After everything had been cleared away, Burton led Noonan down the corridor to a door at the end. Anna hung back at the kitchen door and watched them go. The door opened into a plush, wide drawing room with expensive furniture, book cabinets, black wooden beams across the ceiling and a big colour television set in the corner. Whatever opulence the farmhouse lacked in other areas was certainly made up for in the drawing room. Burton turned on the overhead lights, dimmed them slightly and waved to a telephone over on a shelf.

"Well, I'll leave you to it." He excused himself and left the room. Noonan nodded his thanks and picked up the old Bakelite telephone receiver. He briskly dialled Tristan's telephone number, drumming his fingers on the wood. The phone rang. And rang. Noonan gave it a minute and a half then dropped the receiver back onto its base. At that moment, the lounge door opened, and Anna stepped into the room. She quietly closed it behind her. She stepped up to Noonan.

"'Tom Noonan died a year ago'", she quoted him directly. "I want to hear the rest of it. Right now. And tell me everything."

Noonan sat down on the arm of one of the chairs and hunched over, his hands on his knees. He looked at her seriously.

"If I told you everything," he began quietly, "afterwards, you would turn and walk out of this place and you would never see me again." He shrugged. His voice was hard, matter of fact; it did not invite sympathy.

"I'll be the judge of that," she replied in an equally matter of fact tone. "But I want to hear all of it."

"OK," Noonan replied. He pursed his lips and seemed lost for a moment, as if unsure quite where to begin. Anna went and sat on the arm of an adjacent chair, facing him. She waited. Then he started:

"After I did my National Service and did ten years in the army, I worked for the British Government."

"MI6, you mean?"

He shook his head. "No. MI6 is the acceptable face of espionage. I was involved in the unacceptable one."

He waited for her to react, but she did not.

"I used to work for a man called Lomax. Lomax ran a team of four, which I was part of. There was Drake, Robinson, Bookwalter – and me. It's the kind of department that doesn't advertise itself, or what it gets up to."

"A secret department?"

"Pretty much. More than likely Whitehall isn't even aware of its existence. Lomax controlled us. Lomax gave us the jobs. We never questioned who handed the jobs down to Lomax. We just did them."

"How did you get into this department?"

"I was handpicked along with the other three. When I was in the Territorial Army I was often hand-picked to go on assignments behind enemy lines. These were usually of a classified nature and involved a lot of killing. I happened to do well in these assignments, which is how I came to the attention of Lomax. He set me up with a new place, got me a lot more money than I was on with the army. For a while I was really living the life…"

"What did you do for, Lomax?" she asked quietly.

"If I gave you details of all the jobs that we did, I don't think you'd sleep very well tonight, Anna." Noonan slid back into the cushion of the armchair, gripped his right knee with both hands and looked hard at her.

"Tell me," she insisted.

"Blackmail, murder, death – and all of it perfectly legal. My first assignment involved assassinating a research scientist who was going over to the Russians. That was my initiation test. I passed with flying colours. I knifed his young male lover to death then hanged the defecting scientist in the next room, making it look like a lovers' quarrel. That sort of thing is not uncommon, and no-one would have questioned it.

"A certain politician was becoming too outspoken and building up support where it wasn't wanted. He was politely warned off but to no avail. Then the case was handed over to us. He had a six-year-old daughter who he was keeping in the countryside away from his professional life. He tried to keep that side of his life very private, you see. But we knew. We took the little girl and held her for several days, told him what would happen if he did not back down. Well, he wouldn't listen. The little girl got frightened; poor little thing ran straight into a lorry. I couldn't stop her."

Noonan paused then, reliving the dreadful memory. Then he continued.

"There were jobs that were less distasteful. One time we tracked a German terrorist cell to a farm building in Bedfordshire. They'd taken five hostages, killing three of them. We were ordered to take them all out. We did, and the remaining two hostages were saved.

"The final job I did, Lomax infiltrated an Irish criminal gang that had moved operations from Derry to London and put me in as a sleeper. His people gave me a complete history and I had to learn to live and think like one of these criminals. I had to master the dialect. I did. This organisation ran protection rackets, hard drugs – and were responsible for numerous bank robberies in the Capital. It was on one of these robberies that I found out something that I would have preferred never to have known. We were after political documents from five safety deposit boxes, all located in the same bank. We tunnelled our way in from a furniture shop across the street. It turned out ironically that one safety deposit box we were after was Lomax's. All the secrets of the world were in that box. I didn't see all the contents, but I saw enough." Noonan leaned forward, fixing Anna with a slightly manic glare that slightly unnerved her. He was reliving every moment of the episode. "Lomax runs half the organised criminal gangs in London. They're all in his pocket. He knows everything there is to know. And he's protected by the establishment – which makes him probably the most powerful criminal in the British Isles."

Noonan paused for a moment.

"A little while later, I was jumped, a hood was pulled over my head and I was driven away in a car. When the hood came off, I was in a warehouse, somewhere off the London docks, I guess. My fellow comrades-in-arms had taken me there. Someone had tipped them off that I was an informer."

"Someone?"

"Lomax tipped them off. It had to be him. Somehow, he'd found out that I'd seen inside his box and needed me silenced. So, he turned me over to them. They tortured me for days, weeks even. I lost track of time completely and lost all sense of myself. My mind was turning in on itself. They beat me, used garden secateurs on my fingers..." Noonan held up the scarred fingers on his right hand. "... But I never talked. I was close to death. Mentally I suppose I must have given up. I was in and out of consciousness most of the time. They beat what was left out of me. They kept two of their people with me all the time. Then one night, the place was raided by four other men, all wearing hoods. They killed the two men, grabbed me, and took me away in a car. These four men drove me all the way down to a beach in Dungeness, and then the beating started again. I remember crawling towards the water, thinking, somehow that if I got there, I'd be safe there." Noonan shook his head, lost in his memories. "But I never made it to the water. The four men stood over me. Then the leader removed his mask. It was Lomax. The others must have been

Drake, Robinson and Bookwalter. They'd all been in it together – and I never realised until that moment. Lomax smiled once, raised his gun, and shot me in the chest. They took everything I had from me, all my money…"

"Those wounds on your chest…" Anna wondered aloud.

Noonan nodded. "From the beating. And the big scar is from the bullet. But Lomax made a fundamental error. He went for a chest shot. If he'd gone for the head, it would have killed me. But he didn't. The bullet missed my heart by a fraction and that's what saved my life. They thought I was dead – and to all intents and purposes I was. They left me there.

"Later that morning a fishing boat went past and found me. There was nobody else around. They picked me up and took me to a local doctor who thankfully never kept any records. He took the bullet out and stitched me together. He asked nothing for this, and I had nothing to give him in any case.

"For the next few months, I was a tramp living on the streets. I had no home and nowhere to go. I lost three stone, my hair and beard grew, I bore no resemblance to the person I used to be. I was spat on and kicked. No-one wanted to know me.

"My spirit was broken. But somehow, I managed to make my way back to Tristan. At first, he refused to believe it was me. But then he slowly realised. He cleaned me up, looked after me and started me up again. Anastasia never saw me. I didn't want her to see me like that. So, after that, I started my days of wandering. Everything I owned was on my back. I never stayed in one place long enough to attract any interest. I was a ghost – and that suited me. They were good days. I found peace in my life for the first time. I'd left my old life behind and was able to come to terms with it. Then one day I wandered into Denby."

Noonan sat back in his chair.

"And you know the rest. You and Tristan are the only ones who know the whole story."

Noonan was exhausted. Anna sat there for a full minute, reflecting on everything he had told her. Then she stood up and walked over to him draping herself over Noonan's armchair. She leaned in. He turned his attention to her.

She whispered delicately to him, "Thank you for telling me everything."

She just kissed him once softly on the lips. At that moment, the door opened, and Jacko came in. Anna quickly sat up. Jacko seemed embarrassed. His voice was soft and hesitant.

"I'll show you your room."

Anna smiled at him and got up. When she got to the door, she noticed that Noonan was not following.

"Noonan?"

"I'm going to try Tristan one more time."

She nodded and left the room. Noonan glanced at a carriage clock on the mantlepiece. It was nearly ten o'clock. He went back to the telephone and lifted the receiver. He dialled the familiar number. The ringing tone brayed harshly in his ears but once again there was no answer. Noonan dropped the phone back onto the hook. Where was Tristan? He would just have to keep trying until Tristan eventually picked up. But when would that be?

With nothing further to do, Noonan walked to the door and switched out the lights. He closed the door softly behind him.

21

Noonan found the stairs which led to a long corridor running the length of the house. On the right were various doors leading to the bedrooms and the bathroom. Anna and Jacko were standing right at the end of the corridor chatting. Anna saw him coming and smiled. As he approached, Jacko said to him, "We just thought we'd wait for you because it's a very easy room to miss."

At the end of the corridor to the right was a small alcove. Jacko reached behind him and flipped on a light switch that lit it. There was a solid wooden door in the wall at the end of the corridor, which Jacko pointed to.

"This leads to an outside staircase down to the courtyard." He walked into the alcove. There was a door in the wall on the right. "You're in here," he told them. It was an old door with an old-fashioned latch. He went inside and turned on the light. Noonan and Anna followed him in.

"It's not very big, I'm afraid…" Noonan could find no argument in Jacko's description. The room was about the size of an exceedingly small study. There was a double bed which virtually covered the width of the room. It pointed towards a small window looking out onto the front of the farmhouse.

"We're very grateful for it, believe me," Noonan reassured him.

"You should find the bed satisfactory though," Jacko replied. He seemed uncomfortable and embarrassed, avoiding eye contact with them. There was a door in the opposite wall, though it would have been necessary to climb over the bed to get to it.

"Where does that lead?" Noonan asked.

"To my bedroom. They all have these connecting doors so you can walk between all the bedrooms. None of us ever do though."

Jacko stood awkwardly for a moment with his hands in his pockets.

"Breakfast is at 7.30. Mr Burton likes us to be prompt."

"What's the name of this place?" Noonan asked.

"Reckoning Farm," Jacko replied.

"Where's the nearest town, Jacko?"

Jacko shrugged. "South Molton, I suppose. We're about eleven miles southwest of it on the A361."

There was another awkward pause.

"Well, if there's nothing else..." he mumbled, before climbing over the bed and opening the door into his own bedroom. Anna sat down on the bed and spread her arms behind her.

"I like it here," she said. "These are good people."

"Yeah," Noonan replied, "looks like you got your pig farm after all." He sat down beside her.

"Did you get through to Tristan?" she asked.

"No," he told her. "He's not answering."

"Well, you can always try again in the morning."

Noonan nodded and smiled. He put his arm around her, and she sunk her head into his right shoulder. They closed their eyes. Anna luxuriated in the calm and peace of the moment. It had been a long and frequently terrifying day from which she may easily not have survived. But she had and she felt more determined

than ever to survive everything else that
was to come.

Tristan unlocked his front door at
half past ten that evening and switched on
the hall light. He looked around,
reassured to see that everything was in its
place. Anastasia followed him inside,
closing the door behind her. She leaned
against the wall and exhaled, feeling safe
in the warmth and security of her own
home. Her face was slightly pale. Tristan
looked at her oddly and walked over to her.

"Are you alright?"

"I'm scared," she replied simply.
"Ronnie wasn't exaggerating, was he?"

"Look, you don't have to do this, you
know."

"'Course I'm doing it," she snapped
back immediately. "There's no going back
now."

Just then the telephone rang out
harshly in the hallway. Instantly
Anastasia knew that the call meant
trouble. She looked worriedly at Tristan.
He gave a reassuring nod, walked to the
telephone, and lifted the receiver.

"Hello?"

There was the sound of dead air
coming over the telephone. Then a cheery

but reptilian voice hissed down the phone and into his ear. Tristan immediately stiffened.

"Mr Head. I'm sorry to ring so late..." - the voice sounded anything but - "... but I thought I should let you know that one of your building sites appears to be undergoing a few problems. The car park, Leapale Road."

"Who is this?" Tristan's voice sounded taut, edgy. Anastasia immediately rushed over to Tristan, a concerned look on her face. She leaned into the receiver and tried to hear the voice on the other end of the line. Tristan's grip tightened on the receiver.

"This is Lee Mitchell, Mr Head. As I say, I hope I'm not ringing at an awkward time..."

"How did you get this number?"

"Well, naturally I had to ask a mutual acquaintance. Under the circumstances, he was only too happy to help."

"What the hell are you talking about?" Tristan demanded, a note of disquiet in his voice.

"He was a little uneasy about giving out your private number at first, but he came round eventually."

"There's nothing wrong with my car park at Leapale Road. So, if this is your idea of a joke..." Tristan sounded exasperated.

"I only wish it were, Mr Head. We just happened to be going past at the time. Looked like sheer vandalism to me. A bunch of hooligans, I reckon. Honestly, I don't know what the country's coming to some of the time..." By this point, Tristan was no longer hearing the words. His lips pressed together, and he stared furiously at a point on the wall that he was not seeing. The jocular voice continued. "... Some people just need to be locked away for the good of society. They should never have abolished National Service..."

"I'm going over there now. And if this has anything to do with you..." Tristan's voice was taut, controlled. His emotions had levelled out now. Anastasia gripped Tristan's arm.

"Now there's no need to be like that, Mr Head. I'm just trying to do the right thing here. And after all, I'm only the messenger. And who knows what damage the vandals might do next? After all, we can't keep an eye on them all the time, can we?"

There was a soft click and then the line went dead.

"Mitchell?" Tristan put the phone decisively down. For a moment, neither of them moved and all was silent in the hallway.

"We have to go out," he then said to her quietly.

A row of Victorian houses stretched away along the main road. The headlights of Tristan's Range Rover covered them in a ghostly light as it prowled forward. At the end of the row, there was a T Junction. Tristan waited at the red light. He roared forward as soon as the light turned green. He turned left almost immediately in the next street.

The Range Rover turned onto a piece of land that resembled an abandoned bomb site. Tristan braked. The headlights cut a path of light through the devastation. Tristan and Anastasia just sat there, frozen in the moment, taking it all in. The brickwork of the ground floor of the car park had been thoroughly ploughed through and the fragments of brickwork lay scattered about. The foundations had been ripped up. A cement mixer was lying face down in the mud.

Two diggers had had their windows smashed in. Bricks and debris remained casually spread out all over the ground.

"My God," breathed Anastasia.

"Stay here," ordered Tristan. "Lock the doors."

He stepped out of the Range Rover. He ran over to the diggers, climbed up onto them and looked inside. The insides of both had been ripped out, the machines now useless. Tristan jumped down and stumbled across the debris. He stared up into the black night sky, seeing nothing, his mind a void. Without realising, he bent down, picking up a loose brick. Then suddenly, his face a ghastly mask of controlled fury, he flung the brick away into the blackness. He could not see it as it fell into the shadows, but he could hear it land with a dull, final thud.

Something moved at his side. He turned with a start and immediately relaxed. Anastasia was standing beside him.

"I thought I told you to wait in the car," he told her forcefully.

She came round and faced him. She put both hands on his shoulders and squeezed them firmly. She looked him hard in the eyes and spoke calmly and authoritatively.

"Now listen. This is just the opportunity we've been waiting for. Mitchell's gone too far. And we've finally got a chance to nail the bastard. And we're not letting it go. You understand?"

Tristan opened his mouth, but no words came out. All he could do was simply nod. Anastasia draped her right arm around his shoulders and clamped her left hand on his left arm. Gently, firmly, she led him back to the Range Rover. They got in. The engine growled into life and the vehicle turned round in a wide circle. It turned at the end of the road and disappeared, plunging the pile of destruction back into blackness.

Noonan was awake at 6 o'clock precisely. He had trained himself to wake up at that time and was still in the habit. The need to speak to Tristan was still burning in his mind and he wanted to try again at the earliest opportunity. Anna was lying with her right arm draped over his chest. Her head was nestled comfortably into his shoulder. There was a smile of contentment on her face. She slept quietly and peacefully. He blinked and looked up at the ceiling. The morning birds were just starting their early calls. He reflected happily on another wonderful night with this girl. He had made love to women before, but it had never been like this. She made him feel like a child again, discovering the world in all its wonderment. The terrible years in between with Lomax now felt like an awful nightmare that he was just waking up from. He was certain that he had fallen in love with her, and it confused and frightened him as much as it delighted him. He thought back on how she had explored every part of his body again, reaching a pinnacle with her lovemaking, then moaning softly with pleasure and letting her body drop softly onto his. He carefully lifted her arm and silently got out of bed. He put his trousers and shirt on. He looked down at her sleeping body again. He leaned in and gave her a light, gentle kiss on her left cheek. She sighed happily once and was still. He quietly opened the door and let himself out.

He moved silently down the corridor and crept down the stairs. There were a couple of minor creaks but nothing that would have been heard in any of the bedrooms. He made his way to the drawing room. The curtains were closed, and he turned the lights on. It was chilly in the room. Noonan went straight to the telephone and dialled. There were two rings before the phone was snatched up and Tristan's voice immediately came on.

"Hello?"

"Tristan."

"Tom."

"I've been trying to get hold of you."

"Sorry about that, Tom, couldn't be helped. We've run into some trouble at this end. I'll tell you all about it when I see you."

"Well, I know where the evidence is. Anna told me."

"OK, good. First things first though. We'll come and get you, wherever you are, and then we can take care of the rest of it."

There was a pause. Noonan smiled.

"It's good to talk to you, Tristan."

"It's good to talk to you, old friend. Are you safe?"

"For the moment."

"I'm glad to hear it. Now listen, Tom – the man who's after you: James Michael Jarrett. He was in Northern Ireland around the time of the Troubles. A brilliant soldier but a loose cannon.   He was dishonourably discharged after some incident and now works as a mercenary. Mainly for your girl's husband."

"Yeah, all of that fits."

"Where are you now?"

"A place called Reckoning Farm. Eleven miles southwest of South Molton on the A361."   Noonan reeled off the information exactly as Jacko had given it to him the previous evening.   He had gone over it in his head until it had burned itself into his memory. "It's a pig farm."

"Reckoning?"

"Yes, as in Dead…"

"Can you give me the telephone number in case I need to get hold of you?"

Noonan read it aloud from the disc on the centre of the dial.

"Is the girl OK?"

"She's fine."

"We're coming to get you out of there, Tom.   You just tend to those pigs and keep out of trouble until we get there, you understand?"

Noonan hesitated before speaking again.

"Tristan – it's just you that's coming, isn't it?"

There was a pause and then Tristan answered carefully. "Anastasia's going to want to be there. That's alright, isn't it?"

"Yes, of course it is."

"I'll be seeing you, Tom."

The line went dead. Noonan felt a warm glow in his stomach. Noonan put the receiver down and quietly left the room. There was still another hour and a half until breakfast, and he wanted to spend them with Anna wrapped in his arms.

At seven thirty precisely, Noonan and Anna came down the staircase and entered the kitchen. Burton and the three lads were already in the kitchen. Seth was busy over his stove with an apron on. Baked beans were bubbling in the saucepan and sausages and bacon were sizzling in a frying pan. The aroma of a classic, hearty English breakfast filled the room, and it was irresistible. The four men looked up. Burton nodded and indicated for them to be seated.

"Welcome, welcome. You're punctual. Good, we like that. We've got plenty of work ahead of us today."

The early morning drowsiness seemed to be hanging over everyone apart from Mr Burton, who looked like he had been up for hours and was ready for anything. He was already wearing his outdoor jacket and his boots were on. Conversation was minimal, but the breakfast was succulent and delicious. Noonan had had many excellent breakfasts in many good hotels, but he believed that he had never tasted such a wonderful breakfast in his life. The juices from the mushrooms were luxurious and the bacon was cooked to perfection. There was also scrambled eggs, cooked tomato, and brown toast. Noonan could not let his pleasure at the glorious meal go unmentioned and he congratulated Seth and thanked him. Anna quickly backed him up. Seth looked genuinely surprised at the praise, smiled, and mumbled his thanks.

"Oh, he's a good lad, is Seth," agreed Burton. "Don't know what we'd do without him."

When all the plates had been gathered up, strong, black coffee was served. The smell filled the room and made Noonan feel warm and cosy. Only Anna took milk in her coffee. At the end of the meal, Anna insisted on helping to wash up and put the plates and cutlery away.

"Alright, everyone.   See you outside.   Ten minutes," Burton rumbled, the boss rallying the troops.   He then noticed Anna's totally impractical neat, grey sweater, black skirt, and brown leather boots.   "Oh dear, oh dear," he continued, "I think we'll have to find something a little more suitable than that." He turned to Seth.   "See to it, will you, Seth?"

"Sure," replied Seth, beckoning Anna upstairs.   Anna came down ten minutes later, wearing a khaki sweater, black jeans, and green Wellington boots. Her hair was tied back.   She looked the personification of a farm labourer.   She smiled at Noonan.

Then they all gathered outside.

Tristan unlocked the door to his basement, turned on the light and walked in.   It was a dingy, dusty place stacked with old files.   He was dressed in camouflage jacket and brown corduroy trousers.   There was a steel cabinet against one wall.   He had a small key in his hand, which he used to unlock the cabinet.   He reached in and took out a gleaming, polished Holland and Holland .12 bore shotgun that he used for clay pigeon shooting at weekends. He and Anastasia belonged to a club and often attended meetings. He held it up to the light then slid it into a long, green cloth bag. He fastened the straps. Then he turned and saw Anastasia watching him from the door. She was similarly dressed in a camouflage jacket but wore a pair of blue jeans underneath them.

"You know that's illegal," she warned him quietly. The shotgun licence was in Tristan's name, but the permit allowed him only to use it for his clay pigeon shooting weekends. To be ferrying it around for any other purpose was strictly forbidden, and he was very aware of this.

"I'm hoping it never has to come out of that case," he replied grimly.

"I promise I won't tell anyone if it does." She folded her arms.

"I phoned Justin this morning," he told her. "Asked him to look after things while we're away."

"How long did you tell him we were going to be gone for?"

Tristan shrugged. "A few days."

She nodded. "Well, I'm ready when you are."

He picked up the bag containing the shotgun and followed her out of the room, turning out the lights as he did so.

22

At eight-o-clock, the door to Rectory Farm opened and Jarrett peered out to look at the dawn. He checked up and down the track, but there was no-one in sight. He limped out slowly, shutting the front door behind him. He carried in his hand a bunch of keys and a map. He limped as fast as he could round the side of the farm building to where he expected to find a grey Land Rover. It was where the farmer had told him it would be, and Jarrett found himself smiling. Things were beginning to go his way again. The trail had opened for him and it would now be only a matter of hours before he caught up with the man and the girl. He walked with a spring in his limp.

He found the correct key and got into the Land Rover. For a few moments, he just stared ahead of him, down the gravel track. His mind combed over the events of the previous twelve hours.

Jarrett had demanded a meal and got it, a functional meal of stew and potatoes, but it gave him the strength he needed. The man had given him no problems and had played along with him. The wife however had whined incessantly and pleaded for their lives. Jarrett had quickly tired of her and could feel the compunction growing inside him to kill her when the time came for it. The bleating bitch had been asking for it. Jarrett had no feelings about this. Some people just had to die, and the sooner the better.

After the meal, Jarrett had demanded use of the telephone. He had laid the gun across his thigh as he had dialled with his left hand, leaving his right hand free to go for the weapon if he needed to. He dialled the telephone number that he had memorised but had never had to use until this evening. It was a private number for Mitchell. If he spent more than forty-eight hours on a job, Mitchell liked to be telephoned with a progress report. This was the first time he had ever had to make such a call. He felt sick at having to do so. He would just have to make Mitchell understand. And in any case, he would have the job completed by the end of the following day. Of that he had no doubt. He could guarantee this to Mitchell. The phone had rung twice before

Mitchell had abruptly snatched it up. He sounded angry and tired. Jarrett had explained the situation to him, explained about the man who had temporarily escaped with Anna, which had led to a temporary setback. He had explained that he would have everything fixed by tomorrow evening...

"You've blown it, Jarrett!" Mitchell had suddenly snarled. "You were supposed to have this wrapped up two days ago! Now I've got to come down there myself and sort it out. So, get back here now. You're fired!" The last two words had been yelled down the telephone. Then there was a sharp click, and the call was over.

For a moment, Jarrett sat staring ahead of him, seeing nothing. The man and the woman stared back at him in horror. Then he let his head fall forward into his hands and he let out an animal-like wail. This had intensified into a scream and he had then suddenly grabbed the telephone and thrown it hard against the wall. The unit smashed on impact and dropped onto the carpet, its bell tinging as it did so. The receiver lay sprawled across the floor. Instantly, Jarrett had snatched up the gun and forced the couple upstairs with him. He had made them attend to his injured thigh.   Mitchell's words had echoed deafeningly in his mind and the anger had started to throb horribly through him.   He knew right then that he was going to kill the couple.   That way at least he could control the anger long enough to get the job done.   The couple had a first aid box and had cleaned up the wound, applying antiseptic lotion and bandages to cover it.   The wife at least had made a thorough job of dressing the wound.   The man had stood there silently while all this had been going on, his face a mask of quiet misery and defeat.   He had ordered them to bring him a strong alcoholic drink, and they had found him brandy, which warmed his body and fuelled his strength further.   It had taken the whole night for Jarrett's wounds to be properly tended to.   Waves of sleepiness had washed over him all the way through the night, and his eyes had felt heavy, but he held the man and the woman at gunpoint as he forced himself to stay awake.   The anger helped to keep his mind focussed.

At 2am Jarrett had then ordered the man to find him a map and to mark off where the truck had been heading for, keeping his wife hostage.   This he had done, with no complaint and no arguments.

Then at 7am, he had ordered the man to check the Land Rover and make sure that it was in good working order. While he was outside, Jarrett had ordered the wife to lie down on the bed. She had broken down in tears then and had begged him again not to kill them. She pleaded with him just to go, promising that neither of them would ever inform the police of what had taken place. It was possible that she was telling the truth, but Jarrett's mind was made up. He made her lie on the bed. Then he had taken a pillow and covered her face with it, pressing down. He had heard her muffled moans and her body had writhed on the bed for half a minute before finally becoming still. Once again, the anger inside him started to die away and his mind felt clearer.

Jarrett had been waiting for the man behind the front door. As soon as he had re-entered the house, Jarrett had stepped out from his place of concealment, seized him, and quickly snapped his neck. He gently lowered the body to the floor and took his keys. He had found a cellar just off the hallway and deposited the two

bodies down there. Then with nothing left
to do, he had left the farm.

Jarrett examined the map and
worked out the route to Reckoning Farm.
He folded the map then, laid his Sig-P210
on top of it, and started the engine.

Fifteen minutes later he was
crashing along the country lanes. The
waves of drowsiness were coming over
much stronger now and he repeatedly had
to shake his head to rid himself of them.
His body was craving for rest. He had not
slept for over a day. He forced his eyes
wide open and stared defiantly out at the
road ahead. He would finish the job, no
matter what Mitchell's instructions were.
And he would kill anyone who got in the
way of that. His fingers gripped the
steering wheel fiercely and his foot
rammed the accelerator. He was driving
too fast! He needed to slow down! He took
his foot of the accelerator.

All too late...

He took a tight corner and his body
immediately recoiled. A green Morris
Minor appeared around the corner in front
of him, going at high speed. It filled the
entire windscreen. Jarrett swore loudly
and heaved the steering wheel down to the
right. The Land Rover careered off the

road and smashed into a large oak tree with a sickening, final thud. An elaborate spider's web of splintered glass spread across the windscreen.

Jarrett immediately felt shock and numbness spreading across every nerve in his body. The three seconds it had taken to crash played over and over in his mind in slow motion. All sound was gone. He had no idea how long he had stayed like that.   It may have taken him a few minutes or perhaps a lot longer to shakily climb out of the Land Rover and examine the damage. The front of the vehicle was an unsightly wreck. The front right-hand corner of the vehicle seemed to have been entirely smashed off.   Jarrett tried the ignition, which coughed, spluttered, and died. The vehicle was no longer of use to him.

Quickly, he staggered to the other side of the road. The Morris Minor lay overturned in a grassy bank. Shattered glass lay sprinkled across the tarmac and in the grass. Getting down on one knee, he peered into the car. The window was down. It was a girl inside, maybe as young as eighteen.   Brunette, long hair, curly. Bespectacled.   Her face was turned to his and she seemed to be trying to say something to him.

"He... he... he..." She spluttered in between sharp gasps of breath. Jarrett could only look at her in horror. It was impossible to tell the extent of her injuries. Then she took her last breath and was still. Jarrett took in the dead girl for a few more moments and then stood up.

She had been so young...

He made his way back to the Land Rover, grabbed his map and gun, and began to limp quickly away from the scene, the bile rising in his throat as he forced himself onwards.

The sun was coming up on what promised to be a crisp, clear autumn day. Burton walked alongside Anna out towards the pens.

"You'll be working with Seth over in the west pen," he told her. "You'll find some raw vegetables over in the barn to feed the animals. Seth will show you what to do."

"Mr Burton," she turned to him, "I was wondering if you might allow Seth the night off and let me cook you all something this evening. I'd like to."

"Well, I'm sure Seth would appreciate that very much. So would I."

Seth called over to Anna. "We're over here!" She joined him and they walked to the barn. The others peeled off until Noonan was alone with Burton.

"Let's have a look at the Land Rover then," Noonan suggested. Burton led him round to an open garage containing a tractor and the Land Rover.

"What's wrong with them?" Noonan asked him.

"Something to do with the engine and the gearbox with the Land Rover. That tractor's been out of action for two months, no idea what's wrong with it."

"What tools have you got?"

"Here, I'll show you." Burton opened a drawer on a wooden working area. He pulled out a large toolbox. Noonan opened it and pulled out the various tools.

"This is good," he told Burton. "This is everything I need. You can leave me to get on with it."

"If you can get these things working, lad, then you can definitely stay for supper tonight. Right, then…"

Burton started to leave.

"Mr Burton?"

Burton stopped and turned.

"Yes, lad?"

"My friend Tristan should be coming to collect us either today or tomorrow. Then we'll be on our way."

Burton nodded. "You must do whatever suits – but fix the vehicles first, if you can."

"I'll see what I can do," Noonan replied.

Burton nodded once and walked away.

Noonan worked on the vehicles for the next six hours, getting his hands dirty, checking plugs, leads, examining the gearbox, taking it apart and putting it back together. The hours sped past him, so involved was he in the work that he was doing. He could feel what a hot day it was outside for the time of year. Quite soon he began to feel the sweat forming on his forehead, but he was enjoying his work and was happy.

At half past two, Noonan turned the ignition key and the Land Rover coughed into life. He gunned the accelerator and the engine growled in response. He worked the gears and found that they were in good order. He let the engine run for a few moments to warm it up. He went to the tractor and began to work on it, his face now covered in sweat and dirt. The problem with the tractor was easier to find and fix. The combustion chamber was not receiving the fuel from the injector. The sparks were just not coming. Noonan wondered if a new injector would be needed, but upon extracting it from the engine, discovered that all it needed was a good clean. Noonan took a rag, dipped it in some oil, and cleaned it. That did the trick. Very quickly, the tractor was roaring into life alongside the Land Rover. Noonan turned the engines off.

He walked outside at half past three just in time to catch the last of the afternoon sun. It was now low in the sky and bathing the farmland in a golden glow. Noonan walked through the courtyard and down to the fields. He found Seth and Anna in one of the pens. She was sitting down in the mud, feeding piglets. She was looking down at the piglet in her left arm and laughing. Noonan felt the late afternoon sun warming the side of his face. It was a glorious, golden moment and he realised then that everything he wanted in life was right here.

He approached the fence. Anna turned to him and smiled.

"How are you all getting on?" he asked.

"Why don't you come in and join the party?"

"Oh no, I'm staying right here!"

"This lot are going to be leaving us in a few days unfortunately. They're about ready," Seth informed them.

Noonan saw in the middle of the pack the piglet Anna. He recognised her from the splash of orange on her back. He suddenly felt a pang of regret, remembering the journey she had made with him in the back of the truck and how he had got used to feeling her warm, soft body on his stomach. Noonan shook the feeling from him, realising how absurd it was. He had killed many men in his previous life, usually without remorse. So, what difference did one little piglet make? This was all Anna's fault. Whether he liked it or not, she was changing him, and not always in ways he could comprehend.

He found Mr Burton and told him that he had fixed his vehicles. He was rewarded with a simple, "Good lad", and then it was the end of the working day. The now orange sun dropped below the horizon, and they all went in.

Tristan's Range Rover cut through the wild landscape as the dying rays of the sun chased him. The exhaust fumes from his vehicle hung in the air.

Anastasia sat in the passenger seat with an ordinance survey map of North Devon spread out across her knees. She had been navigating since they had entered the county.

"We stay on this road for a bit, maybe another ten miles. Then we should see the A361," she informed him.

"We're making good time," he replied.

They continued in silence for a few minutes. Then Tristan leaned forward in the driving seat and peered into the distance. Anastasia saw it too.

"Tristan," she started.

"Yes, I see it – there's someone in the middle of the road, coming right at us…"

Tristan continued to peer at the figure coming towards them. As he approached, he could see that the figure was desperately waving his arms in the air at them.

"What the hell…?" he wondered.

"Maybe he needs help," Anastasia suggested. "Should we stop for him?"

Tristan did not reply straight away. The figure was now only one hundred yards away, then less...

Then Tristan was able to make out the face. It took a couple of seconds to register, but then Tristan was gripped by a blind panic. The man in the road was desperately trying to wave them down.

"My God!" he said under his breath. Then in a loud voice he shouted to her, "Get your head down!"

"What?"

"Get down!"

Anastasia did as she was told.

"That's Jarrett!" Tristan bellowed. He slammed his foot on the accelerator and tore towards the figure. Tristan could see the eyes widen in the white face and then the realisation hit him. His hand went inside his jacket pocket and the black metal came out. He raised his arm but only had time for one shot. He fired, the bullet tearing a hole through the engine. Then Tristan's Range Rover was bearing down on him. Jarrett jumped to the side and the Range Rover roared past him. Picking himself up, he lumbered into the middle of the road and began firing again at the disappearing vehicle. Anastasia buried her head in Tristan's lap and

Tristan leaned heavily over the steering wheel. He heard no shots but could feel one of Jarrett's bullets smash into the back door. Then they were away.

Tristan straightened up and checked the rear-view mirror. Jarrett had become an indistinct dot by now and soon was out of sight altogether. Anastasia sat up again.

"Are you alright?" Tristan barked.

"I'm fine," she replied.

Steam was pouring out of the engine now and obscuring the road ahead.

"Damn it!" Tristan swore. He could feel the power in the engine dying slowly away. "Come on!"

Anastasia looked at the map. "How far now?"

"Fifteen miles – maybe."

"We won't make it all the way in this," he told her. "We'll just have to try!"

The Range Rover roared defiantly on down the road.

The black telephone on Mitchell's desk rang sharply. He had a red, a green and a black telephone. The black telephone was for his most private calls, and only two people knew the number. He had been waiting for this call for the whole afternoon. Three hours earlier he had stopped at a telephone box and dialled the number he had been told to use only in emergencies. The usual bland, anonymous voice had answered, and Mitchell had asked for Galbraith. The line went dead. Then the familiar, dry, sardonic voice of Galbraith came on. Mitchell had explained his problem and had asked for assistance.

"Go back to your office and wait there. We'll ring back at five o'clock," the voice of Galbraith had instructed him. And Mitchell had done as he had been told. He went back to the office and at five o'clock on the dot the telephone had rung. It was a call he could not afford to miss. He had needed to go to the toilet for the last ten minutes, but he had forced himself to hang on until after the call. You never got a second chance with these people.

"Have you got a pen?" Galbraith asked.

"Yes."

"Then get this down. Reckoning Farm. Eleven miles from South Molton, North Devon. You were lucky that Mr Head is a person of interest to us right now. Remember to leave the place tidy."

At that, the telephone line went dead.   Mitchell put the phone down and scribbled the address out on a note pad with a black felt tip pen.

After showering and changing, everyone congregated in the kitchen at half past six.   Anna had been busy in the kitchen.   When they were all sitting down, she pulled out of the oven a superb Quiche De Cabinet.   Earlier she had explored the kitchen and found flour, butter, ham, green and red peppers, cheese, and eggs, all that she needed for a quiche.   She had often made these for herself back in Denby and making them had always relaxed her. She laid the quiche down on the table and the five men immediately burst into a round of applause.

"I think this calls for something a little special," rumbled Burton. "Seth, see what you can find in the cellar.   Bring something good."   Seth returned with a 1931 Chateau d'Yquem, which meant nothing to Noonan, despite Burton assuring him that this was one of the great wine years of the century.   Noonan smiled politely, but as far as he was concerned, it looked like red wine and tasted like red wine.   Anna's quiche was magnificent however, and Noonan had watched her slicing it with enormous pride.   The supper was as rewarding as the previous evening, made especially so following a hard but good day's work.   The conversation generally followed along the same lines: bikes, the day's work, and possible future trips to the cinema. Everyone had one glass of wine except Burton, who quickly knocked back three. He was clearly a man indulging a passion. It made him louder, he laughed a lot more, made jokes, and was occasionally on the cusp of becoming argumentative and abrasive, though he never quite did. When all the plates had been gathered up, he gave a deep, satisfied belch, cupped his hands behind his head, and leaned back on his chair.

"Seth, go and get the guitar," he ordered him boisterously.   Seth looked down, embarrassed.

"Yeah, go on, Seth!" jumped in Reuben.   After sufficient pressure had been put on him by all three of the men, Seth reluctantly shuffled away to get his guitar.   He appeared again and took his seat, tuning it.   Reuben and Jacko withdrew towards the window, where

Reuben picked up the cards, cut them and started dealing.

"We'll do 'Men of Harlech'", suggested Burton.

Anna came round and sat down next to Noonan. After Seth had tuned the guitar, he began to strum softly. All other noise died down in the room and all was still. Then Burton started to sing in a rich baritone the Welsh words to Men of Harlech.

It was not a sweet voice and it cracked with all the bitter experiences of life that had shaped it. But it carried with it a rousing strength and defiance and the melody seemed to hold a particular poignancy for Burton. Noonan began to feel it too. For a moment, he was somewhere else in his mind. He felt Anna take his hand and hold it. He turned to her. She was smiling into his eyes and he smiled back. He put his arm round her and pulled her to him. Noonan reflected that if there was a more beautiful language in the world than Welsh, he was yet to hear it.

The sound of the doorbell suddenly buzzed harshly through the farmhouse. The spell was immediately broken. Seth stopped playing. All was suddenly quiet.

Noonan turned to look at the door. Burton looked puzzled and somewhat melancholy. The doorbell buzzed insistently once again.

"Who on Earth could that be?" murmured Burton, now rather sozzled. "Go on, Seth." Seth carefully laid the guitar down on the stone tiles. Suddenly, there was a palpable tension in the room. Noonan wondered if it was Tristan at the door. But this seemed the wrong time for Tristan to be arriving. It was now nine o'clock. Knowing Tristan as he did, he knew he would have either arrived much earlier in the evening or hung on till the following morning. Noonan immediately sensed danger. If it was not Tristan, then who? Could it possibly be Jarrett? Had he found them again? Noonan began to worry internally and wondered if he should accompany Seth to the door. There was something out there in the darkness, and it was coming for him. Perhaps it was finally here. Seth got up and moved to the door. Noonan found himself going with him. Seth went to the front door. Noonan took up a position slightly behind it so that he could get a good look at the unexpected visitor before they saw him.

Seth opened the door. A familiar voice sounded from outside and Noonan immediately relaxed. It was Tristan's voice. But there was an edge to it that he had not been expecting.

"Sorry to arrive at such a late hour," he heard Tristan announce. "My name's Tristan Head. This is my wife Anastasia. Is Tom Noonan here?"

Seth said nothing, just stood back to let them in. Tristan and Anastasia walked in. Noonan's heart lifted to see them both. Tristan then noticed him and turned. Noonan's relief was immediately dampened when he saw the expression on Tristan's face. His skin was pale, and he had seemed to be walking for some time, as there was sweat on his face. He looked relieved to see Noonan but was not smiling.

"What is it, Tristan?" he asked him urgently.

"Tom," he answered. "He's out there…"

23

"He's out there?" Noonan felt his body tauten.

"Not right outside. But he's close."

"Tell me."

"Jarrett. We encountered him on the way down. He was on the road. He shot at the car. It got us to within five miles of where we needed to be before breaking down. We had to walk the rest of the way. Luckily, we'd brought some insurance of our own." He tapped the Holland and Holland on his shoulder. "We had the map, but it was virtually impossible to read it – it's as black as sin out there. Well, we made it eventually, as you see. A little bit behind schedule."

"Are you both OK?"

"Well, we're here," replied Tristan. It was then that Anastasia walked up to Noonan and put her arms around him. She kissed him once on the cheek.

"Hello Tom," she said softly. "We've missed you."

"I've missed you," he replied, looking at her then at Tristan. She moved away from him. Noonan was suddenly aware that Burton had appeared behind them both and was standing in the kitchen doorway. "This is Mr Burton," he told them. "He owns this place."

"Richard Burton." Burton came forward with his arm outstretched in greeting.

Tristan moved forward to meet him.

"How do you do, Mr Burton? Tristan Head. This is my wife Anastasia." They all shook hands.

"Welcome," he said. "You look like you've had quite a time getting here."

"Well, things didn't go as smoothly as I had planned."

"Perhaps you'd like some coffee? We've just made some."

"That's the best offer I've had all day," Tristan smiled. "We'd love some."

Burton led them through to the kitchen.

"I'm sorry about this, Mr Burton," Noonan apologised. "Tristan had a little trouble getting here. I'm not going to lie to you, but his car was shot at by the man who's after us. His Range Rover is on the road five miles away.   It's possible that he doesn't know where we are, but just to be safe, I think we should be gone by first light.   I've one last favour to ask.   I need Reuben to drive the four of us to Tristan's Range Rover.   I'll have to do a job on it. But I've imposed myself on you long enough, I think."

"If anyone comes here looking for a fight, they can have one," growled Burton. "I was with Monty out in the desert for three years.   I know a thing or two about a good fight, son."

"Let's hope it doesn't come to that," replied Noonan.

Burton just put his arm on his shoulder and ushered him into the kitchen. Jacko and Reuben looked up from their cards as the others came in.   Anna stood up.   Tristan approached her.

"Anna."

"Tristan?"

He offered his hand, and she took it.

"I'm delighted to meet you at last. This is my wife, Anastasia."

Anastasia came forward and shook her hand. Anna looked up into Anastasia's large, emerald eyes which sparkled with warmth.   She felt as though she were looking up at an older, more successful sister.

"Hello, Anna."

"How do you do?" she replied quietly.

Anastasia turned to Noonan and gave him an appraising, conspiratorial smile. Anna caught this and turned to Noonan. He was smiling enigmatically back at them both. Anna could not interpret Anastasia's smile or what lay behind it.

Tristan turned to Burton. "I'm sorry to impose, but would you mind letting us stay till the morning?"

Burton shook his head.

"You can take our room," Noonan suggested. "I'm going to be downstairs keeping watch."

"You think I'm going to be able to sleep with just you on watch?" Tristan's face had regained its natural colour and his eyes were alert and full of humour. "Not on your life, I'll be down here with you."

"I'll be down here too," Anna told them. The three of them then turned to Anastasia, who casually folded her arms and looked at them.

"I'm not sleeping on my own. So, it looks like we're all going to keep watch tonight," she told them haughtily.

Burton said, "We've got three shotguns in the cellar. You're welcome to borrow one."

"I'd appreciate that," Noonan replied.

"I imagine you know how to handle one. Being a mechanic, and all."

"Just another tool of the trade."

"That's what I thought. I'll be back in a moment."

Burton suddenly appeared to be entirely sober again. His eyes were watchful, alert and his body erect. He walked briskly out of the room. Reuben and Jacko got back to their cards and Seth busied himself with the coffees.

"How do you take your coffee?" he asked Tristan and Anastasia.

"Black, please," replied Tristan,

"I'll have milk in mine," confirmed Anastasia. Seth poured the coffees and handed them carefully to them. At that moment, Burton entered the kitchen again with a shotgun under his arm. It was another Holland and Holland. It had visibly been well maintained.

"I've given it a drop of oil, so it should handle quite easily."   Burton handed the shotgun to Noonan.   "Try these," he added, also giving him a box of twelve cartridges.   "And just in case he manages to slip past you, I'll be watching from upstairs. Nothing gets past me. Not around here.   And if there's nothing else, let's have some coffee."

"What are we going to be doing?" Reuben asked, looking up from his cards.

"Sleeping,"   Burton   told   him. "Between five of us, we should have the whole place covered."

"No way, Mr Burton. We work this place, we live here. You're not leaving us out of this."

"As you wish, lad."

Anastasia stepped out of the room and entered again carrying Tristan's shotgun.   She broke the chambers open and reached into the pocket of her camouflage jacket. She pulled out two red cartridges and slid them into both barrels. She decisively snapped the barrels shut again.

"Anastasia shoots better than I do," Tristan told Burton.

"At little pieces of clay that go flying through the air. I've drawn the line at shooting people," she replied coolly. "So far."

There was silence in the room from this moment on as everyone drank their coffee. When they had finished, Noonan stepped forward.

"Let's get on with it, then."

The luminous dials of the clock on the mantlepiece in the drawing room pointed straight upwards for midnight. The only sound in the room was its soft clicking like the legs of an insect on a wooden board. Noonan was sitting in one of the kitchen chairs looking out of the window at the black courtyard outside. Burton's shotgun was resting across his knees. He had a switchblade in his back pocket, which Reuben had given him before they had all shuffled out of the kitchen. "A holdover from my younger days," he had told him pointedly. "You can have this. You'll probably be needing it more than me." Noonan had thanked him. As a last resort, it might just save his life. Sitting next to him on one of the other kitchen chairs was Anna. She was looking out into a black void. There was no movement and nothing to see. She tried to focus on the black courtyard, but her mind continued to wander. She kept thinking about the look that had passed between Anastasia and Noonan. It had been there for less than a second. But it had been there. What had it meant? It had contained a secret message for Noonan that only he could have understood.

She turned to him. "Anastasia's very beautiful, isn't she?"

Noonan did not take his eyes off the courtyard. "I suppose so, yes."

"How did she and Tristan meet?"

Noonan frowned. He had wanted and expected Anna to go to sleep on the sofa, but she had insisted on sitting alongside him. This was not the time for this kind of conversation. He needed all his concentration.

"She was his personal secretary."

"Sounds a bit like my story," Anna replied. "Only Anastasia's marriage worked. Mine didn't."

Noonan could not keep the note of irritation out of his voice. "No, it certainly didn't". It sounded harsher than he had meant it to, and he instantly regretted it.

"I'm talking too much, aren't I?"

Anna could not keep the hurt of out her voice.

"No, of course you're not."   He reached over and took her hand.   "You should sleep, you know."

"I can't."

"You could take over for me later on."

She squeezed his hand.   Noonan took comfort from the knowledge that everywhere was covered.   Tristan and Anastasia were watching the back. Burton and his boys were covering from the upstairs.   They sat there in silence as the hours steadily, slowly, relentlessly ticked by.   But they continued to hold each other's hand.

One o'clock...

Two o' clock...

Three o'clock...

Rrrring- rrrrrinngg!   Rrrring-rrrrinngg!

Anna practically jumped out of her skin.   The sudden harsh ring of the telephone in the dark silence of the room was shockingly loud.   She turned and looked at the telephone, but Noonan never took his eyes away from the window.   He whipped the shotgun into his hands and his body tautened.

"Stay still!" he ordered her.

The phone continued to shriek in the darkness. It felt as though it was ringing out across the courtyard and into the darkness. Noonan could swear that if there was anyone out there in the night, they were sure to hear it. Then the ringing stopped, and Noonan breathed a sigh of relief.

Ten minutes later, a floorboard creaked outside. Noonan wheeled round in a crouch, the shotgun snapping up and pointing at the living room door. Anna darted behind Noonan and peered over his shoulder. She could feel her heart thumping in her chest. Noonan stroked the trigger, preparing to squeeze it. Then there was a soft tapping on the door.

Noonan held his breath. Then a familiar voice called to him from the other side of the door.

"It's Burton. We need to talk."

"Come in," Noonan called out softly.

The door opened slowly, and Noonan could make out the dark shape of Burton positioned out in the hall.

"I'm coming in," he said softly. He walked softly in and Noonan got back to his seat, watching the courtyard again. Anna went to the sofa, leaving her chair for Burton. He took it.

"That was my friend the Chief Inspector on the telephone," he started, his voice sounding heavy and serious. "Kilgariff. My friend and colleague Don Wiseman, and his wife, have both been found dead. They lived at the farm where Reuben first picked you up. A neighbour found them in the cellar a couple of hours ago."

As Burton related his story, Noonan's body stiffened, and his eyes explored every murky nook and cranny of the courtyard outside. It had to be Jarrett. Was he out there already?

"It sounds like it could be the work of the man who's after you."

"I think it's Jarrett. I also think he's already here," concluded Noonan.

"I believe he is," agreed Burton.

Jarrett had driven the truck hard through the night. He had found it parked in a layby late in the evening. The driver, a goods transporter, had parked there to grab a few hours kip. That had made it easy for Jarrett. Having walked for hours, his legs at the point of being unable to move any further, this was his opportunity. He had peered in and seen the dark shape of the driver asleep at the wheel. He had tried the door but, sensibly enough, the driver had locked it from the inside. Jarrett had started banging incessantly on the window and calling for help. The driver had hesitated before unlocking the door. Then Jarrett had whipped it open and shoved the gun under the man's chin. The man had called out briefly and Jarrett had dragged him out of the truck. He had then smacked him across the head with the butt of the gun. And then he smacked him again. And again. And then some more. The anger, which had been building up terribly over the course of the day as he had walked painfully, had suddenly reached a terrible crescendo. The body had dropped to the tarmac and lain still, never to get up again. Jarrett had then climbed up into the truck and driven away.

It was the early hours of the morning, pitch black and he had encountered no other vehicles. There was no guarantee that the man and the girl would be at the farm when he got there, but he felt sure that they would be. He had to stop several times to consult the map. Luckily, there was a torch in the truck that he could use to read the map with. He went wrong three or four times the closer he got to Reckoning Farm. At one point, he had travelled five miles down a B road in the wrong direction before he had pulled in, checked the map, and realised his mistake. His Sig P210 pistol was on the passenger seat beside him.

Then, at half past two, he found the entrance to Reckoning Farm. He instantly snapped off the lights in the truck and pulled over into a layby. He was now sitting in pitch blackness. The farm was up there, nearby on the top of a hill. Jarrett picked up his Sig P210 and shoved it into the pocket of his overcoat. He opened the door and stepped out into the blackness.

He reached the bottom of the drive and looked up. His quarry was in the farmhouse at the top. He would be dead by the end of the day. The anger was still eating into him like an acid. Jarrett silently ascended the drive.

"He'll wait for daylight," Noonan advised Burton. "He won't make a move until then."

"He won't know that that we've got this place completely covered. If he tries to break in, we'll blow him apart," Burton replied.

"He won't break in," Noonan emphasised. "He'll wait till I'm alone and vulnerable. Then he'll make his move."

"But you're not alone and vulnerable," argued Anna.

"Then I'm going to have to be," he snapped. "Because that's the only way we're going to get him. We'll have to trap him."

"How are you going to do that?" Burton wanted to know.

"When is first light?"

"Oh, about six forty-five."

"That's when I'm going out. And he must see me leave. I'll go out to one of the fields and start working. As far as he's concerned, I'll be all alone. But I'll be needing one of you to cover me."

"This is my farm," Burton replied. "I know it like the back of my hand. I'll go."

"No," Anna interjected from the sofa. "I'm the one he's after. I'm going."

"Anna," Noonan said, "I need someone very capable to be watching my back. Mr Burton knows his way around here and he's got a much better chance against this man. We're dealing with a professional killer, cold and ruthless as they come."

"It takes one to know one," Anna shot back.

"He's right, Anna," Burton told her. "I was in the war as a young man. I still carry those scars. And you don't forget what the army teaches you."

"You think I can't do this?" Anna challenged them. "It has to be me. I'm responsible for all of this. I'm going."

"No, Anna! Mr Burton goes. And that's final!" Noonan fixed Anna with a hardened glare. Anna sat back, folded her arms, and looked away, anger flashing across her face. Noonan looked over at Burton and nodded his thanks.

"There's a pathway leading to the fields covered by hedges," Burton advised Noonan. "This leads to a small copse looking out across the main field. From there I'll have a good vantage point and Jarrett won't see me. I'll be taking that. Now there's a fence that needs fixing in that field. You can work on that. He'll need to see you working or he'll smell a rat."

Noonan nodded. "I'll leave by the front. As I say, I need him to see me leave."

Burton looked at him dubiously. "Are you absolutely sure about this?"

"It has to be this way."

"Fair enough, then."

"By the time the boys find out what's going on, I'm hoping it will all be over." Noonan paused. "Can you keep watch here?" he asked Burton. "I just need to let Tristan know what we're doing."

Noonan and Anna moved silently through the hall and into the kitchen. Tristan and Anastasia were watching through the kitchen window. Tristan had the shotgun in his hand. He turned in readiness at the sound of the door opening. He relaxed when he saw it was Noonan and Anna.

"What's up?" he asked, looking at his watch. It was four o'clock now.

Noonan explained their plan to Tristan and Anastasia, updating them of the situation.

"You're absolutely mad," was Tristan's immediate verdict.

"Tristan, it's the only way."

But before Tristan was able to ask any more questions or make any further objections, they were already making their way out of the kitchen and back into position.

It was six forty-five in the morning.

Noonan and Burton stood in the hallway by the front door.

"Well, good luck, boy." Burton offered his hand and Noonan took it. The sound of a car coming up the drive suddenly stirred in the morning air. Noonan looked through the hallway window.

"Are you expecting anyone at this hour?" he asked Burton urgently.

Burton shook his head. "No."

"Give me a shotgun," Noonan ordered him. Burton nodded. He went away and came back with one, handing it to Noonan.

A pale blue Land Rover appeared around a corner and parked directly outside the front door. The front doors opened, and two men got out. The driver was young, lean, and hard. He wore an expensive overcoat. The man who got out of the passenger side was older, and similarly dressed. He looked around and smelled the air. Tristan came out of the kitchen, crouching low.

"What's up?"

"Do you know them?" Noonan asked.

Tristan took a quick look out of the window. "That's Mitchell!" he exclaimed.

"And that's another of his shady associates, Remy De Sica."

The back door of the Land Rover opened then, and three tough looking thugs jumped out, dressed in camouflage and donkey jackets. They all wore savage grins. They were immediately familiar to Noonan. The last time he had seen them, they were coughing up blood on a back street in Denby. Their ugly bruises still showed.

"I'm going out the front," Noonan told Tristan and Burton. "See if you can get round behind them. They're probably armed."

"What are you going to do?" Tristan wanted to know.

"Keep them talking," Noonan replied.

Tristan was about to argue but Noonan was already opening the front door and stepping out to meet the men.

<u>24</u>

The five men were spread out in the front yard facing Noonan in a semicircle. Mitchell was in the centre, Remy to his right.

Noonan pulled the door to but did not close it. It would be his only line of retreat if there turned out to be any shooting. He sincerely hoped there would not be. He had not forgotten that Jarrett was around somewhere, and that bothered him considerably more than the five men standing in front of him now. The three thugs had their right arms hidden behind their backs. It was obvious that they were hiding firearms there. He held the shotgun in his right hand, pointing at the ground. He looked from left to right at the faces of the men. He came back to Mitchell, who was standing calmly with his hands in his overcoat pockets.

"Good morning," Mitchell greeted him. "I'm glad to see we're not the only ones up bright and early.   Who am I speaking to?"

"Tom Noonan."

"Tom Noonan," Mitchell repeated, processing the name. "Well, Tom. I would wager that you're the fellow who's been running around with my wife and causing me a lot of aggravation."

Mitchell waited for Noonan to reply. When he did not, he continued.

"I'd like to see my wife, Tom.   So why don't you just pop back inside and bring her out to me?   We've come a long way to see her."

Noonan shook his head.   "I can't do that."

"Oh.   And why's that?"

"If she wanted to come out and talk to you, she would.   But somehow, I don't think she's going to.   Besides, it's not my house."

"Look, Tom..."   Mitchell looked at the ground and casually kicked a stone away.   "I'd like to keep this civilised if possible."

"So would I."

"Then why don't you just bring her out to me?   You can do it.   It won't cost you anything."

"And if I don't?"

"My boys are all armed. All five of them. And there's only one of you. And there's no need for anything like that, is there?"

"That's up to you. Anna can come out. But first you'd have to get back in your car and drive on out of here. Anyway, I've met these three before and the last I saw of them they were bleeding all over the pavement in a fishing village. If your plan was to try and get past me, you needed to come with better material than this."

Mitchell's face had remained confident and buoyant. Now it suddenly hardened, and his eyes turned cold.

"They've been longing to meet you again, Tom. Show him, lads."

The three thugs whipped their arms up, levelling their sawn-off shotguns at Noonan. It was entirely as Noonan had predicted. What he did not, and could never have predicted, is what happened next. Two shots exploded across the yard, blending seamlessly into one. The two thugs to the left of Mitchell both fell forward, blood gushing out from their heads.

Mitchell and Remy were already running, pulling guns out of their overcoats as they looked desperately around for cover.   The third, bulky thug with the triangular sideburns remained frozen to the spot. He raised his shotgun at Noonan, a look of sudden fright on his face.   Noonan instantly whipped his shotgun up to his shoulder, aimed and pulled the trigger.   Blood exploded from the thug's chest and his body fell backwards, landing in a heap.

Mitchell and Remy scrambled behind their Land Rover and crouched down with their guns raised above their heads.   Remy had a Walther PP in his gloved hand, and Mitchell was nervously clasping a small, silver Beretta M1934. Both men looked anxiously around. Mitchell's face particularly had turned pale, his look of calm confidence suddenly gone.   Noonan scrambled back inside the house, levelling his shotgun through the crack in the open front door.   He levelled his shotgun at the Land Rover.

"Mitchell!" he called out across the yard.   "We've got four shotguns!   Give it up!"

Mitchell's voice cracked across the yard venomously.

"You've just killed three of my boys, Noonan!"

"Not me, Mitchell. Jarrett got two of them! He's here right now!"

"Jarrett?" Mitchell looked wildly around. "Jarrett! What the hell are you doing here? I fired you yesterday!" He turned to Remy. "Come on, let's take him!"

"He said it was Jarrett out there!"

"Yeah, well, what did you expect him to say? Come on!"

"No, forget it! This is nuts! Those guys over there are dead!"

"You backing out on me now? Is that it?"

"Too right, I am! I'm not dying for you, Mr Mitchell!"

"Right, you're finished!" Mitchell shouted furiously as he rose from the car and started firing over the roof. Remy joined in a second later. The two guns together sounded like a series of firecrackers being let off randomly. Two bullets tore through the front door and another smashed the glass out of the hallway window. Noonan jumped back, slamming the front door, and moved to the window. He felt the jagged shards of glass drop like knives onto his back. When the shooting stopped, he rose with the shotgun, aimed it, and fired through the shattered window. The report from the shotgun exploded like a clap of thunder across the yard. It blasted a huge, gaping hole in the side of the Land Rover. Mitchell and Remy ducked down again.

Suddenly Tristan Head's voice rang out behind them. "Alright, that's enough! Drop them!"

Mitchell and Remy wheeled around, raising their guns. Burton stood inside the open doorway of the barn building behind them, Tristan down on one knee at his elbow. Both had their shotguns raised and were pointing them steadily at Mitchell and Remy. They both froze. Remy immediately dropped his Walther and it landed with a soft thud on the stone ground. Mitchell's gun remained pointing in Tristan's direction.

"And you, Mitchell. Drop it." Tristan's voice was low and controlled.

"Well, well. Look who it isn't," Mitchell sneered at him. "I love a day out in the country, don't you, Tristan?"

"Just put it down," ordered Tristan firmly. Mitchell threw the Beretta gently into the air. It clattered to the ground a few feet away.

"He's still out there! We need cover!" called out Remy, fear rising in his voice.

Burton scanned around the yard and along the rooftops. All was quiet and nothing moved. He raised his shotgun in readiness. "Come now! Quickly!"

Mitchell and Remy ran crouching towards the barn. No shots rang out. Tristan and Burton stepped back into the barn and let them pass. A side door stood open that Tristan and Burton had used to access the barn undetected. A rectangle of light spread along the stone floor. Tristan raised his shotgun again and covered them. "Right, sit over there in the corner, both of you. And keep quiet." Remy had his arms slightly raised as he backed over to the wall. Mitchell moved with him, looking disgustedly at Tristan. They lowered themselves to the ground.

Noonan ran back through the house. He encountered Anna and Anastasia on his way to the back door. Anastasia held a shotgun in both hands.

"What's happening out there?" she asked desperately.

"Stay here, both of you!" Noonan ordered them.

Noonan stopped at the open door, scouring the open country outside. He hurriedly reloaded. All was quiet. He ducked outside and ran around the side of the farmhouse building, all the while pointing the shotgun in readiness.

Tristan watched Mitchell and Remy inside the barn while Burton carefully surveyed the yard. He then turned back into the barn. A flicker of movement suddenly appeared at the side door. Burton raised his shotgun and hurriedly aimed.

"Look out!" he bellowed. But his warning was drowned out by a deafening explosion, which echoed around the walls of the barn. As Tristan turned towards the door, swinging the shotgun round in an arc, a bullet tore through the right side of his chest. His body spun and fell back. The shotgun in Tristan's hand roared as his body fell back, ripping a jagged hole in the cast iron ceiling. Then the shotgun smacked to the floor and Tristan's body landed messily alongside it.

Jarrett stood languidly in the doorway, the Sig P210 levelled straight at Burton's stomach. Burton stood frozen, his shotgun pointing at the ground a couple of feet away from Jarrett's feet.

"Throw it down," ordered Jarrett. Burton did so and raised both his hands in surrender. He felt his entire body go numb. He was unable to move. Jarrett calmly indicated with his gun to move over to Mitchell and Remy. Burton stood to the right of them. Jarrett moved smoothly into the barn, checking it over. He crossed to Mitchell and Remy and stood over them, the gun at his side.

"You've really blown it this time, Jarrett!" Mitchell spat. "This was supposed to be a straightforward job! You blew it! This guy's been running circles around you. So, I have to come down here and sort it out for you! You've failed, Jarrett! Failed!"

In a flash of movement, Jarrett's arm shot up and the black metal roared. Remy's head flew back against the wall, a bloody hole through the centre of his forehead. Mitchell looked at Remy, his mouth open in horror. No more words came out. Then his body began to shake, the terror throbbing through it. Jarrett ran the gun down Mitchell's body. Mitchell watched it as though he were watching the fob watch of a hypnotist.

"You should have left me to finish the job," Jarrett said simply. He fired again, the bullet drilling a hole above Mitchell's right knee. Mitchell let out an agonising scream, staring stupidly at the blackened hole. Scorch marks appeared on the fabric of his suit trousers. Mitchell doubled over in pain, whimpering. Jarrett turned away from him and stepped towards Burton. Burton's eyes shone with fear, then quiet acceptance.

"Please," he muttered quietly, hopelessly.

"The man and the girl," Jarrett said softly. "Where are they?"

Burton's mouth opened but no words came out. Mitchell continued to whimper and whine in agony. A few feet away, Tristan gasped in pain, holding his side as blood seeped through his fingers.

"Where are they?" Jarrett asked again.

"Right here," came the voice from the side door. Jarrett stiffened. He glanced over to it. Noonan was crouched there, his shotgun pointing straight at him. Jarrett smiled for a moment...

... Then with lightning precision his arm shot up. The two firearms exploded simultaneously, the noise as loud as a crack of thunder. Noonan gasped as the shotgun flew out of his hands, burning his right arm viciously. At the same time, Jarrett felt his right shoulder burst into flames.   He examined it, aghast.   His shoulder was a blackened, bloody mess. He screamed at the top of his voice in pain and fury.   He looked back at the doorway, but the man had gone.   He ran to the door and looked out.   At first, it seemed as though the man had disappeared.   But then he saw him, running hard across the garden towards the fields.   Running away! Tasting victory in his lungs, Jarrett jumped through the door and down into the garden.   He ran after his quarry, leaving one dead man, and two others bleeding to death and writhing in agony back at the barn...

The shots had sounded like a series of angry pops from the corridor of the farmhouse, but every time another one had gone off Anna had flinched.   Anastasia had stood by the back door with the shotgun ready in case any unwelcome intruders found it.   Reuben, Seth, and Jacko stood in the corridor with their backs pressed against the wall.   Anna gripped the side of a hall table, waiting for another pop but finally, there was no more shooting.

Anastasia whispered "OK," to Anna.   Anna and Anastasia approached the back door and looked carefully out.

The three boys followed them. Anastasia stepped carefully out with the shotgun raised. Nothing moved. She beckoned to the others and all five ran to the barn. Anastasia was the first to look in.

She gasped and her hand flew up to her mouth. She saw her husband writhing in pain on top of a thick puddle of blood, a fearless adventurer who now knew nothing but fear. She saw a young, carefree, defiant face suddenly turning old. She saw the lifeless body of Remy, propped up against the wall like a stuffed doll, a final look of bewilderment permanently frozen on his face, a face that would never now get old. She saw Burton bent over Tristan. He had removed his hunting jacket, rolled it up and stuffed it under Tristan's head. He had also removed his sweater and was pressing it into Tristan's side to stop the flow of blood. She heard him speaking softly to Tristan but could make out no words. She did not take in Mitchell. Her eyes had taken in too much already. The acrid smell of death hung heavily in the air. She dropped the shotgun. Behind her the three boys ran in. Burton heard them and turned.

"Help me move him!" he shouted, his voice cracking with emotion.

Anastasia and the three boys rushed in. Only Anna remained outside. She shuddered and turned away. She looked out across the garden, then into the field beyond it. There was a small copse beyond the field. She saw the two men running, both obviously terribly hurt, like broken insects, towards it. Noonan had never looked to her more alone and vulnerable. Up until now he had been her protector. Now she was to be his. She picked up Anastasia's shotgun and raced furiously after the fleeing figures.

Jarrett could see Noonan's figure disappearing into the copse. He saw his dark shape flashing between the trees before he lost sight of him. The sweat was pouring into his eyes. They stung terribly. The pain in his thigh and his shoulder burned through him, but Jarrett was too caught up in the moment to register it. His breath was coming out in agonised gasps. Then finally he was in the copse and looking carefully around. He had him! And he was unarmed! He could feel how close he was to the end of his quest and the thought made him almost reel with pleasure. He carefully moved through the trees, the Sig P210 probing carefully ahead of him.   He moved silently, like a ghost, through the trees.

Nothing moved ahead of him.   No sound could be heard except the occasional flutter of a bird nearby.   Jarrett continued, his senses probing ahead of him.

He never saw it coming.   Never heard it.

There was an explosion of sound and the man leapt out of the bushes at him. Jarrett turned but Noonan was already on him.   He knocked him back, but Jarrett recovered sufficiently to raise the gun straight into Noonan's face.   Both men froze.   Jarrett's face was pale, exhausted but steely.   His shoulders throbbed with a sickening pain.

"I wondered when you'd get here – Jarrett," Noonan told him quietly.

Jarrett seemed not in the least surprised to hear Noonan using his name.

"So, you know my name.   Well, that's very good.   And what do I call you?" Noonan was struck by his voice, which was a reedy, slithery whisper.

"Tom Noonan."

"Tom Noonan."   Jarrett nodded for a moment.   "Well, Tom, given the amount of trouble you've put me through, I'd have to say you were Special Forces."

Noonan shook his head. "British Intelligence."

"Really?" He paused. "I was British Army."

"Yes. I know. They threw you out."

Jarrett shook his head. "They sold me out. Ordered me to a job. Didn't like the way I did it..."

"Sounds familiar."

Jarrett mouthed curled up into a cruel snarl. "So, we were both sold out. And now here we both are."

Behind him, Noonan saw Anna step into view from behind a tree. She came silently forward, holding a shotgun steadily in front of her, pointing at Jarrett's back.

"Where's the girl?" Jarrett demanded.

"Asleep, I should imagine." Noonan looked Jarrett directly in the eye to keep his attention focussed.

"At this time? Never mind, I'll find her." He paused. "No more talk now. Get on your knees."

Noonan gently lowered himself to his knees.

"Now put your hands in your pockets."

Noonan did so. Jarrett took a couple of steps in and raised the gun to Noonan's head.

"I've never been beaten," Jarrett hissed triumphantly. Then he suddenly stiffened. He felt the twin barrels of the shotgun pressing hard into his nape. The girl's voice that accompanied it was quiet, deadly.

"Drop it, you bastard."

Jarrett snorted. "Now what's a nice, well brought up girl like you doing using offensive language like that?"

"You wanted to kill us. Well, now it's your turn. Now drop it."

"Don't make me laugh, darling. You probably don't know one end of that gun from the other. So why don't you just put it down like a good girl? Your husband's waiting for you and I'm to take you back to him." Noonan rose to his full height. "I didn't say you could get up!" Jarrett gesticulated with the gun.

Behind him, Noonan's right hand began to inch towards his back pocket.

"Stop moving that hand!" Jarrett barked. Noonan relaxed his hand. Anna continued to press the barrels hard into the back of Jarrett's neck.

"You can kill me, Jarrett," Noonan told him. "But you'll be dead one second later."

"You believe that?" Jarrett called behind him to Anna. None of them moved for the next few seconds. Then Jarrett raised his gun an inch. In a flash, Noonan jumped to the side and flicked down with his right arm. The switchblade fell down his sleeve and into his hand. He swung his arm up and the knife flashed through the air like an arrow. The sound of Jarrett's gun exploded. Noonan felt the bullet whip an inch past his left ear. Noonan dropped to the ground and looked up. The switchblade had embedded itself firmly into Jarrett's shoulder wound, which had accounted for his aim being off. Blood was gushing out of the wound. Jarrett dropped the gun and Noonan made a dive for it. Jarrett reached behind him and grabbed the barrels of the shotgun, forcing it downwards. The shotgun went off, the shot crashing around the empty fields, as loud as a cannon. Jarrett wrestled the shotgun off Anna and smacked the stock into her face. She cried out and fell to the ground, clutching her face. Jarrett wheeled around to Noonan and brought the shotgun up. Noonan, prone on the ground, grabbed the pistol and raised it. He fired, hitting Jarrett in the chest. The shotgun in Jarrett's hand discharged its second barrel into the air and the sound rocketed around the fields. Noonan fired a second time an inch lower. Jarrett dropped the now empty shotgun. He staggered backwards a couple of steps. Then slowly his body toppled back and crashed to the earth.

Noonan got to his feet and walked to the body. Blood was spreading slowly across the chest. Jarrett's eyes stared vacantly up at the sky. Noonan stood over the body, one foot either side of it. The lips were still parted in a defiant snarl, but the eyes were now at peace. Noonan wondered momentarily whether he was better off wherever he now was. Certainly, his time on Earth would have appeared to have brought him little peace. Then he reflected that he himself could easily now be lying where Jarrett now was. But Noonan felt thankful that he was still at the farm and fully alive. He now was at peace. He shoved the pistol into his belt.

He went over to Anna and helped her up. He examined her face. There was a nasty gash below her left eye where the stock of the shotgun had hit her. It would bruise but it would be nothing serious. He smiled at her wistfully for a moment. Blood was pouring out of his arm and it hurt terribly.

"It's over," he told her.

"I'm sorry," she replied. "I should have acted sooner. I should have blown his head off. I nearly got us both killed."

Noonan shook his head. "No-one knows how they're going to react in a situation like that, least of all the first time. You did fine."

"Well, I want you to know that next time I wouldn't hesitate." She was suddenly looking at him fearfully. In that moment Noonan knew that there was something terribly wrong.

"What is it?"

"It's Tristan," she told him, her eyes filling with tears. "He's hurt, Tom!"

"Oh, God!" The cry was a stab of pain from the heart. She grabbed his hand, and they ran together back through the copse, running harder than they had ever run in their lives.

25

They had run together, hand in hand, across the field. Noonan could feel his heart ready to explode, and he let go of Anna, nothing else existing for him apart from the desperate need to get to the barn. He raced up the stone steps and crashed into it.

The acidic smell of death was heavy now and it hit Noonan instantly. That smell had been an uncomfortable bedfellow for him for most of his life, but he had gotten used to it. But it was never a smell he would have associated with his best friend. It was a smell that belonged to hostile creatures that came from somewhere else entirely. He looked down and saw the bodies crouching on the ground – Burton, Anastasia, Seth, and Reuben. Their bodies obscured Tristan and at first Noonan could not see him. Then Anna came running in behind him and this snapped Noonan into action.

"Tristan!"

Burton turned to see him breaking into the assembled group.

"Give him room!" Burton's voice echoed around the small building. Seth leapt up and stood to one side, allowing Noonan to take his position. Anna remained by the door. Her arms were folded in tension.

Noonan's eyes then took in his friend's condition for the first time. Tristan's face had turned a ghostly white and a thin film of sweat covered his skin. His mouth was slightly open, and his eyes closed. Every few seconds he let out a low moan.

"Get an ambulance, for God's sake!" Noonan yelled out.

He felt Burton's hand gently squeezing his arm and heard his voice gently reassure him, "Help's on the way, boy, don't worry. Jacko's rung ahead for an ambulance."

The pool of blood had spread across half the barn now. Some of it had already started to dry and the pungent, oily smell was already bringing in the insects from outside.

Noonan looked at the others. Anastasia's eyes were wet with tears. Her always glamorous hair now looked dishevelled, unkempt. Reuben and Seth looked at Tristan's face in horror. Only Burton seemed to have kept his wits about him. He was administering care to Tristan as best he could.

Seth came rushing back into the barn at that moment. Noonan looked up. He was carrying a green first aid box.

"Ambulances are on the way!" he called out. "Should take about an hour!"

"Give me the box, hurry!" Burton yelled over to Jacko. He ripped the box out of Jacko's hand and opened it. He took out a roll of bandaging and a bottle of ointment.

"An hour?" Noonan repeated, the situation seemingly turning bleaker by the minute.

Burton turned to Noonan. "I was an army medic in the war. I'll do what I can in the meantime. You just do what I tell you." Noonan nodded.

Burton poured the ointment on the wound. Tristan gasped out in pain. Anastasia leaned forward and began to stroke his hair. The tears rolled down her cheeks freely now. Burton cleaned the wound and handed Noonan a large sterile gauze dressing.

"Press that there!" Burton ordered him. Noonan did so immediately. Burton unravelled the bandaging and started to wind it around Tristan's body. They had to lift his body twice, which caused Tristan to cry out in agony, but it had to be done. Finally, the bandaging was tight and secure.

Noonan looked over at Mitchell, who had passed clean out. He looked back at Tristan. Burton exhaled slowly and straightened up.

"Well, that's about all we can do for now," he intoned gravely. He turned to Noonan, his expression bleak and serious. "You two might want to make yourselves scarce for a while. The police and the ambulances will be here soon and they're going to be asking a lot of awkward questions."

"I don't want to leave him," Noonan replied.

"Go on," Burton ordered him. "I've got everything covered here."

Noonan and Anna were out of sight in the cellar of the farmhouse by the time the first of the two ambulances turned up. Two paramedics quickly jumped out.

"Get this one to the hospital first," Burton ordered them, indicating over to Tristan's body, which they had laid out on the drive. "The other one can wait." Such was the authority in Burton's voice that neither paramedic felt compelled to question it. They loaded Tristan into the ambulance. Anastasia, now having regained some of her strength, accompanied Tristan in the ambulance, staying close to him all the time.

The second ambulance arrived half an hour later and Mitchell was similarly dispatched to Barnstaple Hospital.

Chief Inspector Owen Kilgariff and two subordinates arrived on the scene later in the day. Burton had related the news to Noonan and Anna after they had left. Lots of questions had been asked. The killings had been attributed to Jarrett, though his gun was never recovered. Kilgariff had shaken his head in revulsion and despair. He had never seen so many dead people in one place. One of his constables had staggered to a nearby bush and vomited. He was nineteen years old and looked five years younger. The version of events that Burton had spun had stuck to the facts, with one exception –

Noonan and Anna had fled the scene in the aftermath of the massacre.

It was two weeks before Noonan was able to see Tristan in Barnstaple Hospital. Noonan and Anna had stayed on at Burton's farm in the meantime. Anastasia was staying in a hotel in Barnstaple to be near to Tristan. The two weeks had passed painfully slowly, with the thought of Tristan's condition hanging over everyone like a pall. The mood was glum, but Noonan had distracted himself with hard work. He had fixed the damage to Burton's front door and window and Anna had continued to help with the farm work. At the end of the third day, Noonan, Burton, and Anna had wrapped Jarrett's gun up in polythene and buried it out in the fields. Anna had weighed it briefly in her hand before handing it back to Noonan. It was the final reminder of Jarrett and both Noonan and Anna were glad to be rid of it.

Borrowing Burton's Land Rover, Noonan had driven into Barnstaple at the end of the two weeks. He found the hospital and had been shown into Tristan's room by the young sister on duty.

Tristan was lying there in his own room, a peaceful look on his face. He was still under heavy sedation, but his eyes seemed to recognise Noonan when he walked in and a light seemed to switch on in them. His lips momentarily twitched into a smile. Noonan sat down. He was momentarily lost for words.

"It's good to see you, Tristan," he eventually managed. Tristan gazed back at him distantly.

"And Jarrett?" he whispered in reply.

Noonan leaned forward. "Jarrett's dead," he told him.

"Well, old friend..." Tristan started. Then his eyes shut for a moment. When he opened them again, they had filled with hard emotion. "You couldn't save me that time, could you?"

But before Noonan could reply, Tristan had then drifted back into unconsciousness. Noonan had walked away from the meeting feeling as low as he could ever remember. Then the feeling got worse; the doctor informed him that there was a seventy per cent chance that Tristan would be crippled for the rest of his life. He was also led to understand that Mitchell would be leaving in a wheelchair within a matter of weeks.

The following day, Noonan and Anna had travelled back to Denby. They had gone straight to Anna's cottage. It was the first time that Noonan had been inside, and he could smell and sense her in every room. He had pulled back the refrigerator. A bulky paper folder had been carefully tucked away behind it. Noonan had retrieved this and a day later Anna had presented it to the senior police officer who had approached her so many months ago.

Under police protection, she had backed up the evidence that she had built up against her husband with personal testimony, which was strong enough to secure a conviction. Lee Mitchell's case went before the courts on 1st December. Anna had been summoned to appear in court as a witness against her husband. By 8th December, a verdict had been reached. Lee Mitchell had attended the hearing in a wheelchair accompanied by his lawyer and had been found not guilty. He was wheeled away a free man. It was perplexing and incomprehensible. Anna's evidence had been watertight. Anna had heard the verdict and almost passed out in the courtroom. Noonan had been with her when the verdict had been passed down.

He had offered to take her home, but she had simply pushed him away and staggered out of the courtroom, never looking back. Noonan had known better than to try and go after her.

He did not see her again until the following day.

Mitchell arrived at his Hampstead home later that evening. His Mercedes swept into the drive and braked. The new driver stepped smartly out, opened the boot, and took out the wheelchair. Mitchell got out and manoeuvred himself into it. The driver wheeled Mitchell up to his front door. Mitchell handed him the front door key and the driver opened it for him.

"Pick me up here at midday tomorrow."

"Yes, Sir," the driver nodded. Mitchell then turned and looked at him hard.

"And this evening I want you drunk and celebrating my release, you understand? So, if you go home and watch television, I'll be firing you first thing in the morning."

"Yes, Sir," the driver repeated, a note of confusion in his voice this time.

"Now go on, piss off."

With that, Mitchell had wheeled himself into his vast, ornate reception area and slammed the door in his face.

Mitchell was still feeling euphoric following the result of the hearings. He had beaten them again. He knew that he always would. And in a few months the doctor had said he could be out of the wheelchair. Life was getting back on track. He looked up the white, wide staircase. Lindsay would be around somewhere. Probably she would be down in a minute. But she was usually there to meet him the moment he arrived back. So where was she now?

"Lindsay? Get yourself down here, girl!"

He listened. There was an oddness about the silence in the house at that moment - but for the time being, this did not worry him unduly.

Two soft footsteps sounded behind him.

"Lindsay?"

Mitchell turned around in his wheelchair, a smile on his face. But the smile instantly vanished from his face a moment later. Three shots exploded loudly in rapid succession, the three bullets hitting him squarely in the chest. Mitchell's body was thrown backwards, and it toppled out of the wheelchair. His body rolled once and lay still, the wheelchair landing on top of him.

There was a brief pause and then the footsteps moved towards the front door. A moment later it clicked shut.

The following day, the news of a shooting incident at Lee Mitchell's home had been reported on the nine o'clock news. An unknown assailant had broken into Mitchell's home and shot him three times in the chest before escaping. The dead body of his American girlfriend, Lindsay Schneider, also shot, had been found in their bedroom. Police concluded that it was an underworld killing carried out to silence Mitchell.

It was on the twenty fourth day of December that Noonan walked into the small hamlet called Lower Slaughter in the Cotswolds. He walked briskly and with great pleasure. A small, white fluffy Poochon trotted alongside him. He walked over the small footbridge past the mill and stopped, looking out across the water running through the hamlet, all of it clear and fresh. The Poochon stopped beside him, rubbing up against his leg. There was a look of settled contentment on his face. It was the loveliest kind of winter afternoon. It was half past two and the sun was an orange ball hanging low in the sky. Smoke drifted lazily from a nearby rooftop. The sky was of the deepest blue and layers of frost lay spread across the fields like icing on a grand cake. There was certainly a chill in the air, and it made Noonan feel wonderful. It made him look forward to his evening with Anna, hunkering down in the cottage by the river, both preparing for the Christmas lunch the following day. There was only the two of them to enjoy it, but hopefully they would have stayed in the Slaughters long enough by this time next year to have built up some friendships and have people over for lunch.

Tristan had a friend who spent six months of the year out of the country. He had agreed to loan Tristan the cottage for as long as he was away. Anastasia had quickly moved Noonan and Anna into the cottage at the end of October, and this had been their home for two months, and hopefully would be until the following Spring. Noonan watched the water and reflected on the previous two months, some of the happiest times he had ever known. And today he had a small but rather significant question that he wanted to put to her. She would not be back until the evening, but he was looking forward to seeing her reaction. He was certain in his own mind that it was what he wanted and felt sure that she would want it to. He wanted to be with her for the rest of his life and could not now bear to imagine a life separate from her. The only darkness that had intruded during this time had been the week of the trial at the start of December, which he and Anna had had to attend, and the occasional news of Tristan, whose condition continued to remain uncertain. The last of the visitors to the Mill were coming out and saying their thank-yous and Merry Christmases before it closed. Then the door was closed, and the big lock slid back into place.

"Come along, Tess," he called to the Poochon. The dog had been Anna's idea, and she had come up with the name too. In time, Noonan had grown fond of the little creature. Noonan and Tess trotted back to the cottage. Noonan placed the key in the lock and turned it. Tess ran in and started yelping in delight.

Noonan instantly stiffened. His instincts had not deserted him, despite the relaxed state he had been in for the last two months. Someone was in the house. He felt himself rising to his full height. He walked carefully to the small kitchen on the left. The man – if it was a man – was in the kitchen. Noonan instinctively sensed it. He moved soundlessly towards the door. Tess trotted obliviously over to the narrow staircase and scrabbled away at the carpeted stairs with her little feet. Noonan took a breath, waited for a second, then threw the door open. He wheeled around, his body tense and ready. The empty kitchen sneered back at him. Then Noonan felt the terrible sensation of tiny icicles trickling down his spine. He had experienced this feeling all too rarely, but whenever he did, it meant the worst kind of news. And in that instant, Noonan realised that the man – and he knew then that it was a man - was behind him and armed. Involuntarily his body froze. But where had the man hidden himself? The tiny sitting room area had been completely empty. He had appeared behind him as if he were a ghost. The voice of the man was soft, deadly.

"Stay absolutely still, Noonan. Make any wrong moves and you'll be dead in a second."

Noonan felt his throat go dry and the blood drop from his face. He recognised the voice straight away. It was the voice that had called to him and taunted him from his nightmares. It was the voice of Lomax.

Lomax! How the hell had he tracked him down here? What did he want? Why was he here? There were so many questions rushing through his head. His mind which only two minutes ago had been like a clear blue sky had turned suddenly into a raging storm. Noonan believed Lomax absolutely. He knew that he would kill him in a moment...

... But there might be a way out. There might be that one moment, that one second, where Lomax would drop his guard, and Noonan could take him. He would just have to be patient. And careful. He would have to play out his hand.

"Walk into the kitchen and sit down at the end of the table." Once again, the voice was quiet, professional, assured. Lomax, as usual, had left nothing to chance. He had thoroughly checked the layout of the entire cottage and worked out his movements in advance. Noonan walked carefully into the kitchen and sat down at the end of table. For the first time he looked up at Lomax.

Lomax was positioned in the doorway, his eyes watching him warily. He had a Browning .9mm pistol in his right hand, which was pointing rock steady at Noonan. He looked to Noonan utterly unchanged from the last time he had seen him. He had worked for Lomax for ten years and in all that time he had not appeared to age noticeably. But he had never looked young. He was not a tall man and lacked stature. Yet the power that he exuded whenever he was present in any situation was intensely palpable. He was fifty years old, an Irishman, and yet despite his age, his body was as taut and sinewy as it had ever been. Dark brown hair crawled across a face that looked as though it had been carved out of granite. His deep brown eyes always remained alert, watchful. When Lomax looked at a man, he could read his inner thoughts.

Neither man moved for what seemed like a long time. Finally, Lomax spoke.

"So, you didn't die after all, Noonan. I should have put one in your head, not your chest."

"Why don't you finish the job now then?"

Lomax nodded. "That would be the logical thing to do now, wouldn't it? But it would be a waste."

"A waste?"

"You did too a good job of disappearing, Noonan. I trained you too well. In fact, if it hadn't been for your little telephone conversation with Tristan Head the other night, I wouldn't have been any wiser to the fact that you were still alive."

Noonan pressed his teeth together. Tristan's phone! So, the bastards had had it tapped and somehow his conversation with Tristan had come to Lomax's attention.

"You were the best I ever had," Lomax continued. "And I need you again."

"I don't do that kind of work anymore, Lomax. And I'm not going back. Not for you, not for anyone."

"Come on, Noonan, you have no choice. You never did. From the moment you signed on with me, I owned you. I still do."

"Why now?"

"Because my team was wiped out recently.   Your old friends – Drake, Robinson and Bookwalter."

"My old friends who tried to kill me?"

"Those were my orders, Noonan. You would have done it to any of the others if I'd ordered it."

"What happened?"

"The details are unimportant, but they were on an assignment overseas. They were set up."

"By you?"

A terrible cloud suddenly passed over Lomax's face and for a second he looked like the most terrifying man in the world.   "Don't push your luck, Noonan. You're going to need all of it from now on."

"So, you need a new team?"

Lomax nodded.   "And I'm starting with you, Noonan.   Because, as I say, you're the best."

Noonan shook his head.   "I've already told you, Lomax.   I'm out. Finished."

Lomax's voice remained level, controlled.   "Don't be naïve, Noonan. You're in no position to refuse me."

Lomax's eyes burned through Noonan's and straight through his brain.

They seemed to be on fire. The rest of his body remained still, coiled.

"Why's that?"

"Because I've got conclusive evidence that your girl Anna murdered her husband. I've got the gun and her prints are all over it."

For a second, Noonan almost wanted to laugh. Coming from Lomax, it seemed so desperate, clumsy even. Not even he could make that stick. Could he? Noonan did not laugh, however. He simply shook his head contemptuously. "She was never there, Lomax. You know it. I know it. It'll never stick."

"How can you be so sure?"

"Because she was with me. All the time."

Now it was Lomax's turn to shake his head. "That's not quite true though, is it? There was that one night when she was unaccounted for, the night following the 'not guilty' verdict."

"She's already told me about that."

"Did she also tell you about the gun that she dug up from Burton's farm after you'd buried it?"

Noonan went cold. How the hell could Lomax know about that?

Lomax nodded again. "That's right, Noonan. She dug that gun up and used it to kill her husband."

"You dug it up, Lomax. You killed Mitchell."

"Face it, Noonan. It's the truth. Ask yourself - how well do you really know her?" He paused. "No, the way I see it, she'll go to prison for life for that. And then what happens to your jolly little life in the Cotswolds?"

Noonan spoke quietly as his mind processed the pieces of the jigsaw. "You saw to it that Mitchell got off those charges just so you could set him up and have him killed. Just so you could frame Anna for the murder and guarantee my co-operation."

Lomax shook his head sadly. "She did it. You know it."

Noonan felt the strength draining from him as the terrible possibility became apparent. Or was Lomax luring him in again with one of his malevolent magic tricks? Either scenario was unthinkable.

"You may as well pawn that engagement ring you paid for this morning and get some money for it," Lomax continued. "I doubt you'd be wanting to hold hands with each other across the bars of Holloway Prison..."

Noonan's eyes focussed on a kitchen knife lying dead centre on the kitchen table. If he leaned forward, he could grab it and throw it at Lomax. He could accomplish this within two or three seconds. It was the fastest he had ever done it, and he could do it again now. But Lomax would certainly fire after one second. And even though Noonan's facial expression never altered, Lomax instantly read his mind and knew what he was thinking.

"... Don't even think about going for that knife, Noonan. If I don't walk out of here, that evidence goes straight to Scotland Yard. That can only be stopped by a phone call from me."

Noonan's eyes moved reluctantly away from the knife. "If I go with you, what do I get in return?"

Lomax shrugged. "The girl stays free and lives the rest of her life in peace. The evidence stays with me but stays safe. For as long as you co-operate with me, she'll be fine. I also get to ensure your silence. I know that you know about my other activities. If you say anything to anyone, the girl goes down. It's up to you, Noonan."

"And what about my relationship with her?"

"It ends, Noonan. Today. The work you do for me isn't nine to five. He paused. "Do we have a deal, Noonan?"

Noonan stared at Lomax in stony hatred.

"Let me at least write something to her."

"Be my guest," Lomax replied.

Noonan shuffled around the kitchen, looking for a pen and a sheet of writing paper. Lomax kept him carefully covered with the Browning .9mm. Noonan was suddenly a dead man walking. All over again. He had experienced the very best that life had to offer over the last two months. And in one afternoon, he had lost it all again. Noonan found a biro and a writing pad over on the sideboard. Moving like a zombie, he sat back down at the table and stared at the blank sheet of paper for five long minutes. Then slowly he lifted the pen and wrote very few words. He put the pen down again. Lomax moved carefully into the room, keeping a safe distance from Noonan. Keeping the gun on Noonan, it took him two seconds to read the words that Noonan had written:

"My beautiful, darling Anna –
I must go. I'm so sorry....
Love you always.

Tom"

.

"Time to go, Noonan," he told him. "Come on."

Lomax stood back. Noonan rose slowly from the chair, looked across at Lomax once with veiled hatred in his eyes, and started walking. He walked ahead of Lomax, back through the drawing room, past Tessa, who started yelping in confusion, then out of the cottage, and out of Anna's life. Lomax followed him at a distance, softly closing the front door behind him. The muffled, panicked, desperate barks from Tessa continued to sound from behind the closed door.

There was a brown Ford Cortina parked just around the corner. It reeked of Lomax. Lomax pocketed the gun, got into the driver's seat, and opened the door for Noonan, who got in beside him. Noonan stared ahead of him, his face blank, unreadable.   Lomax started the car and pulled away just as the locals of Lower Slaughter started to come out into the street to begin their Christmas celebrations.

Sitting in Lomax's Cortina silently, Noonan's mind started to go into overdrive. He remembered who he was, who he had always been.   And that very same person would kill Lomax.   And find his evidence and destroy it.

This is what he now had to do.

And he would find Anna again.

And be with her again.

He would.

Printed in Great Britain
by Amazon

59362704R00218